ONE HOUSE.
THREE GENERATIONS.
SIX UNFORGETTABLE CHARACTERS.

Spanning the Georgian, Regency and Victorian generations of the Derringer family, the *Hearts of the Hall* series follows the women who capture the hearts of the Derringer gentlemen.

Get swept away in the romance, misunderstandings, secrets and happily-ever-afters of this faith-based, multi-author series by Philippa Jane Keyworth, Rachel Knowles, and Edwina Kiernan.

FINDING MISS GILES	*Philippa Jane Keyworth*	1780
ENGAGING MISS SHAW	*Rachel Knowles*	1815
RESTORING MISS HASTINGS	*Edwina Kiernan*	1850

HEARTSOFTHEHALL.COM

ENGAGING MISS SHAW

Rachel A. Knowles.

RACHEL KNOWLES

SANDSFOOT

ISBN (eBook): 978-1-910883-05-1

ISBN (Print): 978-1-910883-06-8

Cover design by: Philippa Jane Keyworth

Editing by: Andrew Knowles

Formatting by: Edwina Kiernan

Published by Sandsfoot Publishing, an imprint of Writecombination Ltd, 28, Sunnyside Road, Weymouth, Dorset, DT4 9BL

To my writing partners
Philippa and Edwina
who spur me on

CONTENTS

ENGAGING MISS SHAW

CHAPTER 1

BATH, ENGLAND 1815

*J*ohn growled in frustration. The grey-haired man sitting opposite him winced at the guttural sound.

"Please, can you go over that again?" he said in the calmest voice he could muster. "I'm sure it ought to make sense, but I haven't had your years of experience, and I'm afraid I still don't understand."

"Income on the right. Expenses on the left," Mr Bromley said with a childlike grin. "I learned that when I was just a lad."

"Yes, I've got that now," John said, biting back his irritation. The elderly man cited that rule every time they met. "But how do I tell from these figures"—he waved his hand across the open page—"how the estate is faring?"

"Um...what...what is it you want to know, Mr Derringer?" the steward said, giving him a wary look.

John wasn't sure. He was useless with numbers and after six months, he still couldn't make head nor tail of the accounts. Not that he had tried that hard. He clung to the hope his father would recover and take back the reins of the estate. Then he could return to his life in London and leave all this behind.

He peered at the ledger again, moving his finger down the page, reading the list of expenses. The amounts looked reasonable, but he wasn't sure. He had to confess he had no idea what he was doing.

It didn't help that some entries were difficult to decipher, as the old man's handwriting was growing shakier. Mr Bromley had been steward of Duriel Hall for as long as John could remember, but he would have to be retired at some point. In the meantime, it was safest to rely on his experience. He assumed the elderly man still knew how to run the estate.

John was about to close the ledger when he noticed something. He paused his finger as he read the details of the farrier's bill. Hmm. That was strange. Hadn't he just seen this? Yes. A few lines up, there was an identical entry.

"Why is this amount here twice?"

Mr Bromley went red in the face as he stared at the page. "I...I...don't know."

Darn it. If the man was making mistakes, John would have to replace him without delay. How on earth did he find a new steward?

He squeezed his eyes shut and pinched the top of his nose as if that would somehow make his problems go away. Before he could decide what to say to Mr Bromley, his thoughts were interrupted by the sound of feet running along the corridor outside his study.

John replaced his spectacles and braced himself. The door burst open, and his ten-year-old nephew catapulted into the room. Close behind the dirty schoolboy was a tall, thin woman. She must be the latest in a long line of governesses. What was her name? He couldn't remember.

"What is the meaning of this intrusion?" he said, peering at her through the thick lenses of his glasses.

"Beg your pardon, Mr Derringer," she said, grabbing the boy's arm and pinching him so hard that Philip yelped, "but the rascal slipped through my fingers. He's been fighting with the stable boy again."

John stiffened, his eyes fixed on the woman's pincer-like grip. "Please let go of my nephew, Miss…?"

The woman coloured as she relinquished her hold. "Miss Crewe, sir."

"Ah, yes. Miss Crewe," he said in a measured tone. "Philip ran off again? And got into another fight? Can't you manage the boy?"

She cast a look of loathing at Philip, who had edged away from his governess. "I could if I were permitted to punish him as I see fit."

John's frown intensified. "I won't allow my nephew to be beaten, Miss Crewe. Philip has just lost his parents. Show some Christian compassion."

Out of the corner of his eye, John saw that though Philip's head hung low, his chin resting against his chest, there was a small smile of victory on his face. For a moment, he wondered if he was being too soft on the boy, but then Philip raised his gaze to meet his. The desolation in the depths of his nephew's eyes reaffirmed his stance. He would not let the governess strike her pupil. It must be possible to control a ten-year-old child without beating him into submission.

"Orphan or not, the boy is a slippery dev—"

"Miss Crewe," John barked.

"Call it what you like," she continued, unabashed by John's interruption, "but if you spare the rod, the boy will grow up with nought in his head but sawdust. He won't attend to his lessons, sir, and escapes the moment my back is turned. What is more, he locked me in the schoolroom again this morning, and I would be there still if a housemaid hadn't come in to see to the fire."

John let out a deep breath and his shoulders drooped as he gave his full attention to his nephew. "What have you got to say for yourself?"

Philip hung his head and said nothing.

"You deserve to be punished for treating your governess so poorly."

At his words, Philip's chin jerked up, and he met John's eyes. He held his gaze as if challenging him to carry out his threat.

With a brief shake of his head, John looked away. "Off with you, boy, before I change my mind."

Philip did not need to be told twice. With the flash of a smile at his uncle, he turned and fled the room.

John pushed his glasses back up his nose and studied the woman standing in front of him, a belligerent expression on her face.

"I regret to say, Mr Derringer, that if you persist in this foolish notion that the boy should not be punished for his misdemeanours, I can do nothing with him. I cannot control him, and I certainly cannot teach him anything."

The muscles in John's stomach tightened. He could predict what was coming. Miss Crewe was going to resign. Not this again. Not yet. He must try to prevent it.

"I'm not forbidding you to discipline the boy," he said, in what he hoped was a diplomatic tone, "but I don't want you to beat him. Perhaps you could try a different approach."

Miss Crewe pursed her lips. "I think it's time for you to try a different approach, Mr Derringer. Or a different governess. I'm tired of running around after a child who behaves more like a wild animal than a gentleman's son. If your position remains unchanged, I'm afraid I must give my notice."

"I can increase your wages," John offered. But even as he said it, he knew it would not work.

"You do not appear to be hearing anything I am saying. I cannot be responsible for the child for another day. I wish you well in your search for someone who can control the little wretch without beating him—"

"You have said quite enough, Miss Crewe. You are dismissed."

At last the governess saw she had overstepped the mark and colour flooded her cheeks. She turned on her heel and left the room without a backward glance.

John grimaced. He foresaw a tough week ahead. Last time this happened, the boy had upset John's housekeeper, Mrs Partridge, several times a day. The woman did not care for children—a sentiment he had full sympathy with—and she had hinted more than once that it might be better to send the child to school. John could not deny the idea tempted him.

But Robert would not have wanted Philip to be sent

away from home so young. In this, he would honour his dead brother's wishes. He would have to risk his housekeeper's displeasure by leaving the boy in her care again and pray he found a new governess before Mrs Partridge also handed in her notice.

At least tomorrow was Wednesday. On Wednesdays, they visited his parents in Bath, and it always did them good. His father encouraged him to keep trusting in God and his mother cheered Philip up. She always coaxed him —or, if he was honest, both of them—into a better frame of mind by the time they went home.

John would ask her for help as he had done before. He had full confidence in her ability to rustle up another governess at short notice. Though he was puzzled why he needed another new governess. Why couldn't anyone manage his nephew? Philip behaved well enough for him. Rather sullen, but nothing worse.

"Such a lively lad. Just like his father," Mr Bromley said.

John jumped. He had forgotten the man was still in the room.

Was Philip like his father? John failed to see much similarity between his morose nephew and his fun-loving younger sibling. How he wished he were still alive. Then he wouldn't be in this mess.

What had possessed Robert to appoint him as the boy's guardian? He had known John would squirm at the thought of having a child thrust on him, throwing his ordered existence into chaos. It would have made him laugh—but John doubted his brother would have appointed him guardian if he had foreseen the need for him to step into the role. It had been a foolish whim.

Their married brother would have been the more logical choice.

Robert had been such a good father. John didn't have a clue what to do with a child. How could he ever take his brother's place in Philip's life?

CHAPTER 2

*E*velina Shaw concentrated on her embroidery, her stitches growing increasingly ragged as the interminable conversation dragged on. How could her sister bear it? Mrs Franklin rambled on about how clever and beautiful and advanced her three-month-old son was, as if she were the only woman in the world with a baby that laughed.

That was not the worst of it. Having exhausted her supply of praise for her child, she moved onto the less wholesome topic of the failings of others. Did Mrs Franklin have to relay every snippet of gossip she had gleaned since her last visit? At one point, her voice dropped to an undertone to share a juicy tidbit with Cecilia, which she deemed unfit for Evelina's maiden ears. Not that it made any difference. Her hearing had always been good, and she caught every detail of the rumoured indiscretions of Bristol society's newest bride.

How Evelina wished she still had an excuse to escape from the drawing room. But those days were gone. The boys were both at Eton, and she was no longer needed to tame her sister's stepsons.

At last, Mrs Franklin took her leave, and the two sisters were left alone.

Cecilia glanced at Evelina's embroidery and shook her head. "It's fortunate the boys didn't need to learn how to sew if that's your best effort."

Evelina ignored her sister's jibe. "You won't distract me by your petty criticism of my handiwork. Why do you tolerate that woman?"

Cecilia blushed guiltily. "Mrs Franklin is my friend."

Evelina shuddered. "How can you admit friendship with a woman who delights in tearing another's reputation to shreds? And on such slim grounds. She pounced on the slightest mistake and blew it out of all proportion. Her victim's character will be destroyed before dinner. I hope her husband is understanding enough to see the rumours for what they are."

She paused and fixed her sister with an accusing stare. "You didn't say a word in the poor lady's defence."

Cecilia refused to meet her eyes. "You don't understand. Mrs Franklin is married to one of Bristol's wealthiest men. I dare not risk upsetting her, or I might become her next target, and that would make James uncomfortable."

Evelina opened her mouth to argue that was a poor excuse, but then shut it again. She could not criticise her sister's loyalty to her husband.

"Besides, I like to hear how her son is doing. It helps me to know what to expect," Cecilia said, looking fondly down at her increasing stomach as she ran her hand over it.

"But where was Mrs Franklin's baby? From the way

she talked, I am surprised she could bear to leave her precious son."

"With his nurse."

"Exactly. If I had a child, I would spend time with him."

"She could hardly bring a squalling babe on a morning call."

"Perhaps she should have stayed at home and saved us all from her spiteful conversation."

"Evelina, that's not very charitable. Have some sympathy for her. Her marriage is unhappy. Her parents arranged the match, and her spouse is old enough to be her father. It is not surprising she dotes on her son and grabs at every bit of passing gossip to bring her some amusement. I know it bothers you to hear Mrs Franklin talk about others like that, but I don't think she really means any harm."

"I'm sorry."

"You won't have to put up with her for the next few months. Her husband is taking her to Bath, where she can find entertainment whilst he drinks the waters."

"I don't mean to be grumpy. The truth is, I'm restless. I miss the boys."

"You're not the only one. I miss them too."

"I'm sure you do, but although you're their stepmother, I spent more time with them, preparing them for school and playing cricket and...well...there isn't really anything for me to do anymore. Apart from embroider badly and listen to conversations I don't want to hear."

"Darling, you don't need to do anything. James and I are both agreed that you deserve a rest."

"That's just the point. I hate having nothing to do."

"Then marry and have a family of your own."

Evelina rolled her eyes. She had wondered how long it would be before her sister started promoting marriage again. Why couldn't she let the subject drop? The only two offers Evelina had received were from middle-aged widowers who were clearly looking for a mother for their children, not a marriage partner.

But she could not voice her opinion without upsetting her sister. Cecilia had jumped at just such an opportunity to escape from their aunt's home. Forced on their relative's charity after their father's death, they could never forget they were impoverished relations.

Evelina did not blame Cecilia for accepting James's offer, and she had to admit her marriage had worked out well. James had come to love her, and her sister had found her place in society.

Not every widower, however, was as kind as James, nor half so attractive. Cecilia was the beauty of the family and it had not surprised Evelina that she had drawn the attention of Bristol's most eligible widower. Evelina did not have her sister's looks, and the offers she had received had not tempted her in the least. She was not prepared to take such a risk with her happiness and end up in a miserable marriage like Mrs Franklin.

"Don't look at me like that," Cecilia said. "You're so good with children, it wouldn't be right for you not to have any of your own."

"You forget that having children requires me first to marry, and despite you throwing me in the path of every eligible man in Bristol society, no one with whom I could contemplate spending the rest of my life has asked me."

She heaved a sigh of relief as the door opened, interrupting their conversation. The footman announced their next visitor moments before Mrs Derringer wafted into the room with a baby in her arms. Evelina exchanged a speaking look with Cecilia. Some ladies clearly defied convention and took their offspring on social calls with them.

Mrs Derringer was a vivacious lady of a similar age to her sister. Evelina knew this friend was as talkative as Mrs Franklin, but much more pleasant. It was therefore no surprise when Mrs Derringer launched into speech before she had even taken her seat.

"Forgive me, but I couldn't bring myself to leave Frances at home and I knew you wouldn't mind. There are some people I would not dream of calling on with a babe in arms. Mrs Franklin would not say so, but she wouldn't approve—which is almost as bad as saying it, don't you agree?"

Mrs Derringer turned to Evelina. "Would you like to hold her?"

Without waiting for an answer, she handed her daughter to Evelina and sat down on the sofa next to Cecilia.

"Well! What a to-do. John's new governess has left after little more than a fortnight. She claimed Philip was unmanageable. Tell me, how can a ten-year-old be unmanageable?"

Evelina pressed her lips together, trying not to laugh as she thought of her sister's stepsons before she tamed them. Mrs Derringer had clearly not had much experience of ten-year-olds, and neither, by the sound of it, had John, whoever he was.

"I see you're wondering who this unruly ten-year old is, who has chased off his latest governess, and why he is in the charge of my bachelor brother-in-law." Mrs Derringer leaned forward as though sharing a great secret. "The boy is my nephew, Philip. Poor John inherited him from my *other* brother-in-law, Robert. He and his wife both died of smallpox six months ago and—"

"Oh, the poor boy," Evelina exclaimed.

Mrs Derringer gave her a warm smile. "Quite so. The mystery of it is why Robert made John Philip's guardian in the first place. John. Who doesn't know anything about children. He's not even married, nor ever likely to be, as he spends more time digging up old bits of pot and showing them off to his antiquity-loving cronies than he does in polite society. How he ever expects to meet a lady...

"I digress. The point is, poor John is desperate. I've sent him my best recommendations for governesses, but none of them have stayed beyond a month. They can't control Philip in the least. He keeps locking them in the schoolroom and running away. His mother asks me for another, but I have no more to give. Now, he will have to send the boy to school, whether or not he wants to. Unless you have a suggestion, Cecilia?"

"I'm sorry I can't help you. My sister had charge of my boys before they went to school, and I certainly wouldn't recommend any of the governesses that came before her."

"Tell me more," said Mrs Derringer.

"Cecilia once had a similar problem," Evelina said. "When she wed James, Richard was ten and Thomas a year older. The boys had been allowed to run wild after their mother's death and they were—how shall we put it? —mischievous. The governesses my sister employed failed to curb their high spirits and Cecilia won't mind me saying she was at her wit's end before I came."

Mrs Derringer raised her eyebrows. "Is that true?"

Cecilia nodded. "Quite true, I'm afraid. I became a mother overnight and nothing had prepared me for it. Fortunately, Evelina came to live with us, and she has always been good with children. Within a matter of weeks, she had calmed their behaviour and taught them more than the previous four governesses put together. They even started showing some affection for me, which I feared might never happen. It was such a relief not to have disappointed James, and I might add, it was two respectable schoolboys who went to Eton last September."

"How did you do it?" asked Mrs Derringer, her attention caught.

"Cricket."

"I beg your pardon?"

"Cricket. And battledore and shuttlecock. And anything else I thought of to use up excess energy. It worked wonders."

Mrs Derringer's eyes gleamed. "Perhaps you would consider..."

Evelina found her heart beating faster. She had been praying that God would give her a new challenge— someone else she could help, now her sister no longer needed her. Was this the answer to her prayer?

"Anne, you are forgetting," said Cecilia. "It is one thing for my sister to help me out, and quite another to be hired out as a governess. And to a single gentleman at that. My sister is a lady. It is out of the question."

Evelina scowled at her sister before turning to Mrs Derringer. "I wish to try."

"It wouldn't be proper," Cecilia said in clipped tones, returning her sister's scowl.

"There are plenty of other ladies who become governesses," Evelina said.

"That is because they have fallen on hard times. You have a home here. With me." Her voice was becoming a whine. "You don't need to work for your living."

"I fail to see why that makes a difference."

"Ladies only become governesses when all else fails. It is an arduous life. You'll never find a husband if you lower yourself like that. Are you really so set against marriage?"

"If I found a man who loved me as much as James loves you, I would marry tomorrow. Since I have not been blessed with your good fortune, I must forge my own way. Mr Derringer needs help, and I would like to try."

As their eyes met, Evelina willed her sister to understand how important this was to her.

After a few moments, Cecilia dropped her gaze, and her scowl gave way to a sulky pout. "Have it your way. You are of age. But how will I explain to James that you would rather play governess than remain his guest? Is it so objectionable staying under my husband's roof?"

Evelina's scowl vanished in an instant. She returned the baby to Mrs Derringer's arms and walked over to her sister. Taking both her hands in her own, Evelina looked deep into Cecilia's eyes.

"James has been very good to me. Not every man takes in a spinster sister as readily as your darling husband did. But now the boys are at school, I feel... empty...purposeless. I need to feel useful."

"But I would miss you. How will I cope when the baby arrives?" Cecilia said.

"I will miss you, too, but you won't be alone. You have your husband and a whole army of servants at your disposal, besides your friends. Mr Derringer and his nephew need rescuing. It would be wrong not to go when I think I could help."

Cecilia gave a reluctant smile.

Mrs Derringer seemed to take that as a signal of her friend's consent. Her face lit up with pleasure. "I will write to John at once."

Evelina's gaze lingered on the baby as Mrs Derringer said her goodbyes. A deep longing tugged at her heart, but she brushed it away with her usual common sense. It was pointless yearning for a family of her own when it was out of her grasp. With no dowry and indifferent looks, her chances of marrying a man she could love and respect had never been high.

If she followed this course of action and became a governess, they would be non-existent. She hoped she would not live to regret it.

CHAPTER 3

*I*t had been an interminable week since Philip's last governess had left. How could one boy cause so much havoc? Taking his glasses off, John laid them on the desk in front of him and put two fingers on each temple, trying to ease the dull ache that had settled there.

Right on cue—as if his thoughts had summoned yet more disruption—he heard the sound of feet running in the corridor outside his study.

"But I want to see my uncle," Philip's voice wailed as the footsteps stopped.

"Mr Derringer has more important things to do than deal with a scrubby schoolboy," came the firm voice of Mrs Partridge.

John couldn't agree more. Yet here the boy was again, disturbing his peace. How was he supposed to work with such an infernal noise outside his door? He would never finish cataloguing his collections if he kept getting interrupted.

With gritted teeth, he replaced his spectacles and got

up from his desk. He strode across to the door and yanked it open, ready to snap at Philip, but his angry words were not required. The corridor was empty. His nephew had gone, dragged away by Mrs Partridge.

He breathed a sigh of relief. What a blessing that his housekeeper was so zealous in keeping the boy out of his way.

After shutting himself in his room again, he walked back to his desk. A sliver of guilt nagged at him for dismissing his nephew so readily, but he refused to let it take root.

He thumped his desk in frustration. It was Robert's fault. He should never have appointed him as Philip's guardian. John had never wanted children.

He tore the front cover off the newspaper lying on the desk in front of him, screwed it into a ball, and threw it at the door with as much force as he could muster.

What was he supposed to do with a child? How could he ever take his brother's place in Philip's life? He tore off another sheet of newspaper, and then another, screwing up each page, and firing them like cannonballs at the door.

He looked at the pile of scrunched newspaper projectiles lying on the floor and let out a sigh that seemed to come from his very soul. Of course, he could not replace Robert. He was not—and never could be—Philip's father.

A sharp rap brought him out of his reverie.

"The new governess has arrived," the butler announced, pushing open the door and scooping all John's newspaper cannonballs behind it. "Shall I show her in?"

John fought through the fog that clouded his

thinking to make sense of Mr Partridge's words. A new governess? Was he expecting her today? Why was it so difficult to think?

He had not even looked for a replacement this time, so how did she come to be here? Then he remembered. His sister-in-law, Anne, had written him a letter. She'd found someone. Maybe this woman would be able to manage Philip. He couldn't.

John nodded slowly. "Yes, please show her in, Partridge."

The butler ushered a woman into the room and left them alone together.

John stared at the lady and the lady stared back. There must be some mistake. She could not be the new governess. She was too young. Not just out of the schoolroom, but some years younger than he was himself. None of the previous governesses had been young.

Nor had they been modish. This lady wore the sort of dress his sister-in-law would wear. Her hair was a nondescript brown colour, but instead of being pulled back into the tight bun he had assumed every governess adopted, it was arranged so that a few soft curls fell on either side of her face.

He continued to stare. Though her skin was clear— devoid of the smallpox scars he dreaded—her features were unremarkable. He was tempted to call her plain. But plain or not, she looked more suited to his sister-in-law's drawing room than to teaching Philip. He had been right. She could not be the new governess. There must be some mistake.

"Mr Derringer, I presume," the young lady said, her eyes twinkling with amusement as she thrust out her hand toward him. "I am Evelina Shaw, your new governess."

Evelina. What a pretty name. Wasn't it the title of a novel his mother liked? John gave himself a shake. How long had he stared at her? He took her outstretched hand and shook it.

"I...I...welcome, Miss Shaw."

There it was again—the look of amusement in her eyes. It lit up her whole face, and he wondered why he had thought her plain just a few moments before. She would never be a society beauty, but she was not unattractive.

"I am not what you were expecting, am I?"

John let out a slight noise that might have passed for a laugh. "Forgive me, I am not used to receiving young ladies—especially not alone, in my study."

Miss Shaw chuckled. "This is not a social call, Mr Derringer. I am here to look after your nephew. Besides, I am not so very young. I have been on the shelf for years."

John frowned. Could such a confident lady have lacked for offers? He doubted it. Then again, perhaps her dowry was small. Or non-existent. Few could afford to marry with no consideration of fortune. He wondered if that was the case. He would have liked to know, but it would be impolite to ask.

"Will you employ me, Mr Derringer, or shall I leave?"

John stared at her again. Could this self-assured young female succeed where others had failed?

"Forgive me, Miss Shaw, but you do not look like a governess. What is your experience?"

"I assumed Mrs Derringer had informed you of that. I cared for my sister's stepchildren."

"Ah, family," John said with a shake of his head. "I

fear you will find someone else's children more difficult to manage."

"*You* did not see my nephews before I took them in hand."

"How did you control them?" John asked. "Did you beat them into submission?"

Miss Shaw's entire expression changed in a flash. She looked as if she were about to explode. "I did not."

"What, never?"

"It was not my place. Their father took the rod to them from time to time, but he reserved it for the worst behaviour, and it was seldom used."

"Hmm."

"I trust you do not expect me to beat your nephew, for if that is the case, I will tell my maid not to bother to unpack."

"Your maid?"

For the first time, Miss Shaw lost some of her confidence and blushed. "My sister insisted. For propriety's sake. Mrs Derringer assured me it would not be a problem. I hoped she had already broached the subject with you."

John shrugged his shoulders. "Maybe she did. I don't remember. However, it fuels my original assessment that you are not a governess."

"Would it help if I told you I am not on the lookout for a husband?"

"From my experience, every unmarried woman is on the lookout for a husband."

"I am not. Though not against marriage in principle, I'm not prepared to resign my independence to look after someone else's children for free—and that is the only sort of marriage I have been offered. Although you're not a widower, you have a child that needs care. I'm here to be a governess to that child—so I repeat, without hesitation, I am not on the lookout for a husband."

John stared at her. Again. As Miss Shaw spat out the last word, she met his gaze. Her eyes grew wide with shock, as if only then she realised what she'd said. She covered her mouth with one hand, looking as if she wanted the floor to swallow her up after her outburst.

"Miss Shaw, you are a most unusual lady."

She lowered her hand and bit her lip. "Outspoken, you mean. Forgive me, I should not have said that. I assure you, I do not usually, but the question remains. Will you employ me to look after your nephew or not?"

John stood in silence, trying to decide. He used to decide things so easily, but now... He did not for one minute believe this unusual young lady—for he could not bring himself to think of her as anything but young —could tame his nephew. But he was strangely unwilling to send her away.

Deep inside him, something flickered. Was it hope? He didn't know. Was it dangerous? Probably. But it was the brightest feeling he had experienced in months, and his gut told him to grab it with both hands.

CHAPTER 4

*E*velina hardly dared to breathe as she waited for Mr Derringer to answer her question. What had prompted her to speak like that to a gentleman she had only just met? And not just any gentleman—the gentleman who offered her an escape from the confines of her sister's home.

His gentle goading had pierced her defences in moments—defences she had built up over three years to protect her sister. She had not wanted Cecilia to think she disapproved of her marriage to James. If Evelina were offered such a union, knowing it would be as happy as Cecilia's, she would marry tomorrow. But her sibling's marriage was the exception, and she wasn't prepared to take that risk with her happiness. She would rather remain a spinster.

"All right, Miss Shaw. I will give you a month to prove your worth."

Evelina could breathe again. She was not being sent home because of her outburst.

Mr Derringer rang the bell, and a few moments later, Mr Partridge reappeared.

"Please take Miss Shaw up to the schoolroom to meet her pupil," he said in a voice devoid of expression.

So, he was not even going to introduce her to his nephew. That didn't bode well for him or the boy. But she did not dare challenge Mr Derringer. Yet.

She looked expectantly at the butler, but he didn't move.

"If you please, sir. Master Philip is not in the schoolroom."

Mr Derringer sighed. "Might I ask where he is?"

"I don't know, sir."

"Then you had better put Miss Shaw into your wife's capable hands, and she will have to meet the boy when he returns."

Evelina blinked, unable to hide the surprise and, she had to admit, disapproval of Mr Derringer's cavalier attitude.

"Aren't you concerned your nephew is missing?"

"He'll come back when he's ready. He always does."

Evelina's mouth dropped open, and she was about to confront Mr Derringer, despite her previous good intentions, when he forestalled her.

"Miss Shaw, you do not know the boy. You do not know how my household works and you do not know me. Please keep whatever reproaches you are about to utter to yourself. My housekeeper, Mrs Partridge, will show you to your room."

As he finished speaking, he lowered his gaze to the papers in front of him.

The message was indisputable. She had been dismissed.

Although Mr Derringer's abrupt treatment of her rankled, she could not afford to take offence. She had chosen this life, and must get used to being treated like a governess. With one last glance at her employer's bowed head, she turned and followed the butler out of the study without another word.

He led her down a flight of stairs and knocked on the first door they came to, which Evelina assumed was the housekeeper's room. It opened, revealing a stout, homely woman in her middle years.

"Yes?" she barked at them.

"Mr Derringer told me to bring the new governess to you. This is Miss Shaw."

Mrs Partridge gave a curt nod, and her husband beat a hasty retreat. She looked Evelina up and down as if she were an object of curiosity.

"You are the new governess?" she asked, her tone dripping with disbelief.

"Yes," Evelina replied with the confidence of one used to directing servants all her life.

"You are very young," the woman said, flaring her nostrils as the corners of her mouth turned downward.

Evelina bit back a hasty reply. It would not do to make enemies amongst the staff. She refused to be cowed by the woman's obvious disapproval. Mr Derringer was sceptical of her abilities, but if he saw fit to employ her, it was no business of his housekeeper's to question it.

"I should like to be shown to my room—if you please," she added, trying to be conciliatory.

Mrs Partridge looked as if she had just taken a mouthful of something bitter.

"Certainly, Miss Shaw."

The woman closed the door behind her and led the

way up the staircase to the ground floor. Instead of heading down the corridor toward Mr Derringer's study, they climbed another flight of stairs.

As Evelina followed the housekeeper, she glanced back at the double doors which she supposed must lead to the main drawing room. She noticed there was a motto carved in stone above the doorway:

GOD IS MY HOME

A half-smile crept onto her lips. Mr Derringer doubted her, and Mrs Partridge disapproved of her, but she would trust in God. He must want her here for a reason.

As they mounted a third staircase that led to the top of the house, Evelina's legs ached. Something else to get used to in her new life—lots of stairs. The older woman fared even worse, gasping for air when they reached the landing. Evelina suspected she didn't come up here often. She bit back a smile as she had a wicked thought. The housekeeper would not be so stout if she came up here more frequently.

"You will take your meals in the schoolroom with Master Philip," Mrs Partridge said when she had caught her breath. "You are expected to attend the church service with the rest of the household on Sundays. On those Wednesdays when Mr Derringer takes his nephew into Bath to see his parents, you may have the day off."

She pointed at the door in front of them. "That's the schoolroom, with the nursery to the left and your room to the right." She paused. "The last governess couldn't manage the boy, and I expect you'll do no better. Mr Derringer will soon realise his nephew needs to go to school. In the meantime, keep away from the master's study. He doesn't like to be disturbed."

Without waiting for a reply, Mrs Partridge went back down the stairs.

Evelina watched her go, trying not to let the woman's abrupt departure unsettle her. Did the housekeeper treat every governess with such a lack of respect, or had she garnered her disapproval because of her age?

She opened the door to the right of the schoolroom and entered a small bedchamber where her maid was unpacking her luggage. There was no separate dressing room and having accounted for the bed, closet and washstand, there was barely enough space on the floor for her trunk.

Maggie gave a loud and deliberate sniff. "I've done my best, madam, but I can't fit all your clothes in here," the disconsolate maid said, waving her hand at the tiny closet.

Evelina muttered something reassuring and walked to the window, which she was relieved to see was of a decent size. She smiled with pleasure as she surveyed the delightful grounds. Directly below her were manicured lawns. To the right were the formal gardens whilst on the left, she noticed a bridge. She assumed a river ran on that side of the property, which probably fed into an ornamental lake somewhere out of sight.

She was about to turn away when she spotted a movement near the bridge. Was that a boy climbing down the banks of the river? It must be her pupil. As she watched, he disappeared from view. What a good thing she was looking out of the window at just that moment. If Philip went missing again, that would be the first place she would look.

As she switched her gaze from the picturesque view to her sparsely furnished room, Evelina's smile faded. Her bedchamber was the least inspiring part of Duriel Hall she had encountered. Did this represent how her life would be from now on? Had she made a terrible mistake leaving the comfort of her sister's house?

A sigh escaped before she could stop it. She immediately took herself to task. This was the path she had chosen. To come to Duriel Hall was the right thing to do. Even if her room was no bigger than a cubbyhole and the surly housekeeper predicted she would fail. Not to mention her arrogant employer, who doubted she was capable and appeared so unfeeling toward his nephew. If her situation proved unbearable, she need not stay, but she would prefer to prove them wrong.

CHAPTER 5

*J*ohn couldn't concentrate on the papers in front of him. He could not stop thinking about Philip's new governess. What on earth had possessed him to let Miss Shaw stay? She had no references. No experience outside of the family. A young lady with outspoken opinions who would no doubt destroy his peace.

What was more, she had already passed judgement on him. He'd seen the look on her face. She disapproved of his lack of involvement with his nephew. She thought he didn't care.

Miss Shaw was wrong. He did care about Philip, but how could he replace Robert? The boy needed a father, and John was not cut out for the job.

He was roused from his thoughts by another rumpus in the hall outside his study. Philip again, he assumed. This was becoming a habit—a habit he hoped the new governess would break.

Sure enough, the door flew open, and his nephew

rushed into the room. The boy's face was alight with excitement. He looked so like Robert that John almost cried out in grief. Unable to bear the bittersweet sight, he lowered his eyes abruptly as Philip started to speak.

"Uncle, look what I've—"

"What are you thinking of, boy?" Mrs Partridge scolded, appearing in the doorway behind him. "You're dripping all over your uncle's study."

"But I—"

"Polly, take Master Philip and make sure you clean him up ready for his dinner when he can meet his new governess," Mrs Partridge barked over her shoulder.

A maid appeared from behind his housekeeper's substantial form, took Philip's hand and led him away before John could think of anything to say.

He looked hopelessly on—like a spectator of his own life—as another servant arrived with a mop and bucket and cleaned up the puddle his nephew had made. She disappeared as fast as she had come, leaving him alone with Mrs Partridge.

"I'm so sorry to have disturbed you, Mr Derringer. I hope the new governess is more successful than the last, but my first impression isn't favourable. Too fine for the role, if you ask me, but she'll soon learn her place or leave. You'd be much better off sending Master Philip to school than having this constant change of governesses. At Eton, he'd have the company of other lads. It must be hard for the boy not to meet anyone his age of the right station. Now, I've got a nice roast duck being prepared for your dinner and one of those puddings you are so fond of and—"

"Thank you, Mrs Partridge. That will be all," John

said, more curtly than he'd intended. It niggled him that she was casting aspersions on the new governess. It was one thing for him to have his doubts, but quite another for his housekeeper to voice her disapproval before his new employee had a chance to prove herself.

"Very good, sir."

As the door closed behind her, John wondered whether Mrs Partridge was right. Would Miss Shaw learn her place, or would she leave like all the rest?

A faint glimmer of hope entered his mind. Miss Shaw certainly didn't resemble the others.

Which brought him back to the question he was pondering when Philip burst in. Why *had* he agreed to let her stay? Was it desperation that had prompted him to let her play at being a governess until she gave up? After all, she couldn't do worse than the others.

Or was he so impressed with her confidence that she could manage Philip that he believed she could succeed where her predecessors had failed? No—though perhaps she would surprise him.

He rather thought it was because he had felt more alive during their brief interview than he had for months —and it felt good.

EVELINA REFUSED to allow the size of her bedchamber to dampen her spirits. She would act like the lady she was, even though she was being treated like a governess. Although she dined with Philip, she would change for dinner, as she always did.

"My lilac gown with a Norwich shawl, Maggie. I can't depend on there being a fire in the schoolroom."

"As you wish, madam."

"Don't look so glum. I know my quarters are cramped but—"

"You shouldn't be shut away up here. It's not right."

"Maggie, it's my choice. I chose to come here to discover if I could help. And I'm blessed with the knowledge that if it doesn't work out, I can return to my sister's house. Most governesses are not so fortunate."

"Then I hope it doesn't work out," Maggie mumbled to her back as Evelina left the room.

Ignoring her disgruntled maid, Evelina walked the short distance down the corridor to the schoolroom and opened the door.

A harassed-looking girl, whom she learned was called Polly, hovered just inside the doorway, keeping a lookout for her arrival. The servant bobbed a quick curtsey, and then stood back against the wall as Evelina entered the room. A boy sat slumped in his seat with his elbows on the table, resting his chin on his hands.

The child made no effort to rise or even look up.

Not a promising start.

"Good afternoon, Philip," Evelina said.

The boy jumped as if her presence in the room was a surprise to him.

"It is polite to stand when a lady enters the room."

He did not move.

"Master Derringer, please stand up," she said, raising her voice slightly.

Philip glowered at her as he stood, pushing back his chair so hard that he knocked it flying. Evelina observed he was a sturdy lad, about four feet tall. His mop of brown hair looked as if it could do with cutting, and the belligerent expression on his face did not augur well.

She had to exert her authority now or lose her pupil from the start. Looking him in the eye, she said in a calm but firm voice, "Please pick up your chair."

Philip held her gaze for what felt like an age before bending over to right his seat. He immediately flopped back down on it.

Ignoring the manner in which he had carried out her instructions, Evelina gave him a warm smile. His obedience was a minor victory.

"My name is Miss Shaw," said Evelina. "I am your new governess."

"I know," said Philip, not looking up. "I saw you arrive."

"You did? I didn't think you could see the driveway from here."

"You can't."

"You weren't at your studies?"

"No."

Then it was not her arrival that had caused Philip to flee from the schoolroom. He must have escaped earlier if he had watched her coach come up the drive.

Evelina wondered how much time he had spent away from his lessons since his parents died. It seemed his uncle had left him to run wild, despite the succession of governesses brought in to teach him.

With a nod to Polly, their dinner was served. It was plainer than she was used to, but that was to be expected. She was eating nursery fare now.

Notwithstanding her best efforts, Evelina drew only the briefest of comments from Philip in answer to her questions. At length, she gave up trying to converse, and was not sorry when the simple meal was over, and she could consign her charge into the care of his nurse.

It was not an auspicious beginning, but she refused to be disheartened by her first encounter with her pupil. She would make better progress in the morning. If she wanted to stay, she must.

CHAPTER 6

*D*espite the lumpiness of her mattress, Evelina slept well. She did not stir until her maid woke her at eight o'clock the next morning. With the new day came renewed resolve. She remembered the disbelief she had seen in Mr Derringer's eyes when he had agreed to let her stay and was determined to prove herself capable of teaching his nephew.

She refused to be discouraged that her first attempts at drawing out her pupil over yesterday's dinner had fallen flat. If she could tame Cecilia's stepsons, she must be able to manage a single ten-year-old boy.

Mrs Partridge had told her Philip started his lessons at nine o'clock, so Evelina headed for the schoolroom at a quarter before the hour, expecting to have time to prepare before he arrived. To her surprise, she found Polly hovering inside the doorway, and her pupil already at the table, eating his breakfast.

Or rather, playing with it. He was shredding a piece of toast between his fingers and dropping it on the table, bit by bit. He glanced at Evelina, and then at the mess in front of him, and with one swipe, he swept the crumbs flying all over the floor.

No wonder the housemaid looked harassed if the boy made a habit of creating this kind of chaos.

"Sorry, madam," Polly said, "but Master Philip isn't used to waiting."

Picking her way through the debris, Evelina addressed her pupil before taking her seat.

"Good morning, Philip."

No response.

"Good morning, Philip," she repeated, raising her voice.

"Good morning, Miss Shaw," Philip mumbled, without looking at her.

"Aren't you forgetting something?"

He looked up and glared. "What?"

"To your feet, please."

Her gaze did not waver as Philip continued to glare. After a few moments, he rose from his seat and echoed his muttered greeting.

Evelina nodded her approval and sat down as he retook his chair.

"I trust you enjoyed a good night's sleep," she said as she poured herself a cup of tea from the pot. She was not surprised to receive no answer.

While she drank her tea and ate a slice of toast, Philip stared at her in silence, making her feel like an animal in a menagerie at feeding time. It was a relief when she had eaten her fill and Polly cleared away the breakfast things.

Evelina turned her mind to teaching. As she shut the door behind the maid, she checked the keyhole. She had no wish to be caught napping by leaving a means for her pupil to lock her in—should he feel so inclined—but there was no key.

After perusing the contents of the shelves lining one wall of the schoolroom, she selected what she was looking for—paper, pens and ink.

"I wish you to write me a letter in your best handwriting," she said, "telling me about something you enjoy doing."

"Why?"

"Because I want to see how well you form your letters and to learn about you—what makes you smile."

"Nothing."

"Then tell me what makes you grumpy."

Philip puffed out his cheeks and blew out the air in a whoosh, making his lips vibrate noisily as he did so. He dipped his pen into the ink and wrote, but after a few lines, he stopped.

"This is silly," he said. "You're supposed to be teaching me useful things—things I will need when I go to school."

Evelina raised her eyebrows. "Don't you want to be able to write a fine letter home to your uncle when you are at Eton?"

Philip flung his pen down on his paper, spurting ink all over the page.

"What's the point? He wouldn't read it. He's not interested in me."

The hurt in the boy's voice was unmistakable.

"I'm sorry you feel like that," said Evelina. "I'm sure your uncle would be eager to hear how you get on."

"No, he wouldn't," Philip retorted. "You don't know. You've only just arrived, but you'll be gone soon enough. Like all the others."

Evelina hoped he was wrong. She looked down at the spoiled paper.

"Never mind. Let's find something to soak up the spilt ink and then I'll give you a fresh sheet so you can start over."

She found some blotting paper on the shelves with the writing supplies, but when she turned back to offer it to Philip, she discovered he had disappeared.

Bother. She'd have to chase after him.

Evelina pulled down the door handle, but it didn't budge. She tried again, but it was impossible to open. Her enterprising pupil must have wedged something underneath the handle on the other side.

"Philip! Release me at once."

Silence.

After rattling the handle once more, she beat her fists on the door in frustration. She called out repeatedly for help, but there was no response. Nobody could hear her cries.

There was nothing she could do. She was trapped.

After selecting a book from the shelves, she sat down and waited to be rescued. Evelina hoped she could escape and retrieve her pupil before Mr Derringer discovered he was missing.

⁓ • ⁓

AFTER EATING breakfast alone as usual, John settled himself in his study and tried not to think about Miss Shaw. He couldn't rid himself of the impression that she disapproved of his behaviour—and it irked him.

Determined to lose himself in his work, he opened a

cupboard and took out a shallow, rectangular wooden container and laid it on his desk. It was full of fragments of Roman pottery and tesserae that he'd found on an estate on the other side of Bath, just a few weeks before Robert died. He seemed to have been cataloguing the same one for weeks. Come to think of it, he had. Everything seemed to take much longer than it used to.

He laid one of the pottery fragments on the desk in front of him. Picking up his pencil and sketchbook, he copied the design onto the page. He noted the hue, so he could fill in the sketch with his watercolours later. It was the part he liked least, so he tended to put it off as long as possible.

John flicked through his papers to see whether he'd come across this pattern before. He didn't find an exact match, but it was like a piece Robert had sent him a few years earlier. His brother would be interested to know...

He stopped short. Robert was gone. He would never know.

John leapt from his chair and paced the room. He was not sorry for his brother, who was in a better place, free from the pain of the disease that had taken him.

But he was sorry for himself—and his nephew. They were the ones left to suffer.

Poor Philip. John realised he wasn't doing his duty by the child. It wasn't the boy's fault his parents had died. Or that they had consigned him to John's care. Or that he was so inadequate for the job.

The sliver of guilt he kept pushing down came roaring to the surface. Was Miss Shaw right? Could he do better?

It wouldn't hurt him to show some interest in the boy. He could visit the schoolroom and see how Philip's studies were progressing. At least he wouldn't have to face him alone. Miss Shaw would be there to help. Maybe it would earn her approval.

He mounted the stairs to the top of the house. As he climbed, his heart beat faster and not from exertion alone. How should he enter the schoolroom? He'd never done it before. Should he announce his arrival with a knock or go straight in? It was his house, after all—but no, he would knock.

In the event, his musings were unnecessary. When he reached the top of the stairs, he saw that the schoolroom door handle had been jammed shut by a high-backed chair.

He let out a disappointed sigh. Philip was up to his tricks again. Despite her claims, Miss Shaw could not control the boy any better than the previous governesses.

John removed the chair and opened the door.

"Thank goodness—oh—Mr Derringer," Miss Shaw said, her face dropping as she realised who had rescued her.

"Miss Shaw, where is my nephew?"

The governess's cheeks turned a deep red. "I'm afraid I don't know."

A wave of regret passed over John that his initial assessment of her abilities had been right. His disappointment made his words come out much harsher than he intended.

"You don't know? Miss Shaw, you are his governess. You *should* know. You claimed you could handle my nephew."

She bit down on her bottom lip, as if she were keeping back a hasty retort. "Philip was upset, and he spilt some ink. I turned my back on him while searching for some blotting paper, and by the time I found it, he was gone."

John folded his arms across his chest and shook his head, unable to hide his frustration. "Perhaps if you were more experienced, this would not have happened."

"Wouldn't it? Is it possible that every governess you have employed to teach Philip is as inexperienced as I?"

John felt the heat rising under his collar. "No, of course not. You are the first to come solely on my sister-in-law's recommendation."

"Then how do you explain the fact that Philip has given every single one of them the slip? Perhaps if you had taken the trouble to find out why your nephew kept running away, this would not be an issue."

"Miss Shaw, you have said quite enough. I suggest you endeavour to find Philip before you waste a whole day's teaching."

With these words, he turned abruptly and left the room without giving Miss Shaw any chance to respond.

What right had any woman to bowl into his life and tell him how to deal with his nephew? It was not the governess's position to dictate to him. This was his household, and he would run it as he pleased.

John headed straight for his study, resisting the temptation to slam the door behind him. He returned to his work with renewed vigour if without any genuine enthusiasm. He refused to listen to the niggling doubts at the back of his mind that there might be some truth in Miss Shaw's words.

CHAPTER 7

*E*velina did not waste any time mulling over the injustice of Mr Derringer's scathing words. After grabbing a pelisse and bonnet from her bedroom, she hurried down the stairs after his retreating form. She descended the second flight and headed for the door.

Once in the gardens, she sped along the path she hoped led to the river. It was where she'd seen Philip from her window the day before. It seemed logical to try there first.

Although she'd had no time to explore the grounds yet, she had a good sense of direction and believed she was going the right way. As expected, the trail ended at the stream, but there was no sign of Philip. She stood and waited, hoping that if he were hiding, he would make some noise that would give his location away.

Nothing.

Was it conceivable he was tucked away under the bridge? Was it even possible? She decided she should rule out the chance of his being there before looking anywhere else. Tentatively, she climbed down the bank and edged her way toward the three-arched bridge, stepping on the flat stones that lay in the shallow water, trying not to get her feet wet.

As Evelina reached the left-hand arch, she peered underneath. There was a large rock which made a decent resting place, but there was no sign of Philip—or was there? She crept under the arch of the bridge, bending over to avoid banging her head.

On top of the boulder was a pile of what looked like pebbles. She picked one up to examine it and realised she was wrong. For a start, it was a cube. It was a dull red and made of—what was it? Pottery? Stone? She'd seen some cubes like this in a museum. If she was not mistaken, it was a piece of Roman mosaic.

Had Philip hidden the tesserae here? It seemed likely. Where could he have got them from? A worrisome thought crossed her mind. Had he stolen them from his uncle's study?

Evelina wondered what to do. If Philip were a thief, she would have to tell Mr Derringer. He might not believe in corporal punishment, but such a trait must be caught early, or there was no telling where it would lead. But if she turned Philip over to be disciplined by his uncle without giving him a chance to defend himself, she would have lost her pupil's confidence before she'd had the opportunity to win it.

What a dilemma. She had only been here one day and already she faced a tough choice. Closing her eyes, she prayed under her breath for wisdom about how to deal with this situation.

As soon as she said the words, she realised she knew what to do. She would give Philip a chance to explain. She returned the piece of mosaic to the place she had found it and retraced her steps along the river. Her most pressing need remained unmet. Philip was still missing.

Clambering up the river bank was trickier than climbing down and Evelina caked her boots in mud before she made it onto the path again. Where should she seek next?

What had James's sons done when they were angry or upset? All too often, they'd taken it out on each other. In the early days, she had broken up more than a few fights between them, before she learned to build sufficient physical activity into their daily routine.

Where would Philip find someone to fight? The stables were the most likely place. There was always a boy training to be a groom in her sister's household. She failed to see why it should be different here.

Evelina sped along the path back to the house and then veered off toward the stables. To judge from the grunts and shouts coming from the yard, her guess was correct. The ghost of a smile crept onto her lips. She could retrieve her pupil and resume lessons without incurring more of Mr Derringer's wrath.

As she walked through the archway into the stable yard, she heard the sharp voice of Mrs Partridge. Her heart sank as she realised she'd been beaten to it.

"Restrain your lad now or I'll have him turned off with no reference."

A man, whom Evelina guessed was the head groom, grabbed the other boy by the scruff of his neck and hauled him off.

Deprived of his opponent, Philip almost fell over. He scowled up at Mrs Partridge, who closed her fingers around his arm and pulled him toward the archway where Evelina stood.

"I can take Philip from here, thank you, Mrs Partridge," she said in the most confident voice she could muster. "There's no need to disturb Mr Derringer."

"Oh, I don't think so," she said, shaking her head. "That's not a sensible idea. If he's escaped you once, he'll escape again. I told the master how it would be. The boy needs to go to school, Miss Shaw."

Refusing to relax her vice-like grip on Philip's arm, Mrs Partridge strode toward the house, dragging him behind her. Evelina could do nothing but follow in their wake and deal with the consequences she felt certain her employer would mete out.

She kept a close eye on Philip as they walked, hoping for a clue about what was going on inside his head. He gave nothing away, keeping his gaze on his feet—until they reached the door of Mr Derringer's study. Then he looked up and his eyes sparkled with excitement, as though he were looking forward to facing his uncle, even though he was in disgrace.

How curious. Was that Philip's intention all along— to be taken to see his uncle?

Mrs Partridge rapped on the door, her eyes gleaming with triumph. It was as if she was glad she'd caught Philip fighting again. The woman seemed keen to tell Mr Derringer about it. What had happened to her claim that the master did not like to be disturbed?

"Enter," Mr Derringer said in a long-suffering voice.

Mrs Partridge opened the door and pushed Philip inside in front of her. Feeling helpless that she had failed a second time, Evelina entered the room behind them.

"I apologise for disturbing you, sir, but Master Philip has been fighting again."

Mr Derringer looked up, his brow creased with

concern. He stared first at Mrs Partridge, then at Philip, and finally at Evelina. She held his gaze, refusing to be cowed by the censure in his eyes.

After what seemed like an age, he turned back to Mrs Partridge and fixed her with a questioning look.

"And what, pray, has that got to do with you, Mrs Partridge?"

The housekeeper flushed red. "I thought you'd want to know he'd escaped from his new governess. She's no better than the last at keeping him at his studies."

"Thank you, Mrs Partridge," Mr Derringer said with a sigh. "I know the boy ran away again. But as he has now been found, I suggest you allow Miss Shaw to take her charge back to the schoolroom and resume teaching."

"Very good, sir"—a tightness around her mouth showing how unwelcome his words were—"if that is what you wish. But if he keeps fighting like this, you'll have to send him to school or there will be no peace in your household."

"Thank you for your concern. I'll bear it in mind. And now, perhaps, I can have my study back to myself."

Mrs Partridge left at once, and Evelina followed, tugging a reluctant Philip away by the hand. The housekeeper cast them both a look of loathing before stalking off down the corridor.

Evelina bit back the smile that rose involuntarily to her lips as she saw the woman's discomposure. She had clearly expected Mr Derringer to side with her. It was discouraging that Mrs Partridge was so set against her, but heartening that her employer hadn't dismissed her yet.

She had another chance to prove she could win Philip over. This time, she must not fail.

Evelina was keen to introduce her pupil to some more productive ways of using his restless energy before he got into another fight with the stable boy. After lessons the next morning, she suggested they spend time outside.

Armed with a bat and ball from the schoolroom, she led Philip to a flat area of grass on the nearside of the stream and attempted to interest him in a game of cricket. She soon discovered he differed from her sister's stepsons, who had readily engaged in all the physical activities she suggested.

She tossed the ball at Philip's bat, only to have him miss almost every shot. After half an hour, Evelina gave up.

The following day, she tried again. Having spent the morning wrestling over some mathematics questions with Philip, she tried to play a game of battledore and shuttlecock with him. Her efforts met with a similar lack of success. She couldn't decide if Philip had no aptitude for sport or he just wasn't trying.

"Didn't you play any of these games with your father?" she asked in exasperation when a game of bowls proved as disastrous as her previous attempts at gaining his interest.

Philip shrugged. "Not much."

"Then what did you do together?"

The boy spoke with animation for the first time. "We played in the river."

"What sort of things did you play?"

"We made boats out of paper and raced them. And

built dams—to change the course of the stream, or to build waterfalls. Mother liked waterfalls, so we did that for her."

"Would you like to make boats tomorrow?"

Philip's face lit up. "That would be—" He broke off, his eyes clouded with uncertainty.

"What is it?"

"Do you think Father would mind if I did things with you I did with him?"

Evelina gave him a reassuring smile. "I'm sure he would be pleased."

With the promise of a trip down to the stream ahead, Philip was a more attentive pupil the next day. After a light luncheon, they made a dozen paper boats and went outside to race them down the river.

Philip let out a whoop when his boat beat hers for the first time, making Evelina's heart leap for joy. What a relief to discover the boy hadn't lost his ability to have fun. Her only regret was that his uncle was not there to witness it.

CHAPTER 8

*T*hat morning, as on every other day that week, John sat in his study dealing with estate business, and then cataloguing his collections. Every time he caught a noise in the passageway, he expected Philip to burst in, but he didn't. If he had not known better, he would think he missed being disturbed.

John had not visited the schoolroom again. He had not spoken to his nephew since driving him and his governess to the church service on Sunday. Their words had been few, and John had retreated to his collections as soon as they returned.

His study was beginning to feel more like a prison cell. He mourned the days he could just pack up his bags, climb in a carriage, and travel to explore the latest bit of Roman history someone had uncovered. Now, he could only remember the freedom he once had, before responsibility trapped him inside Duriel Hall. He hadn't planned to give up his carefree existence so soon.

A footman arrived with the day's mail. John sifted through the letters until he came to one bearing his brother's handwriting. His brow furrowed in concern as he broke the seal. Charles rarely wrote to him. John hoped Anne and the babe were not ill. He spread open the single sheet and his frown disappeared as he recognised the florid style of his sister-in-law's hand. He should have guessed. Anne had written the letter, not Charles.

My dear John

How is Philip's new governess settling in? I'm keen to hear from you about Miss Shaw, that I might reassure her sister. Cecilia is one of my dearest friends, and she was none too pleased that I encouraged Evelina to come to your aid. I hope the extra maid is not an inconvenience to you. It is a trifle irregular, I know, for a governess to bring her own, but it was the only way I could persuade Cecilia to agree.

Despite her lack of experience, something about Miss Shaw instilled me with confidence, and I saw at once she would make a pleasant addition to your household. Besides the wonders I trust she is working on Philip, I'm sure her witty conversation keeps you on your toes. Indeed, I expect having female company at the dinner table lifts your spirits, which have been understandably downcast of late.

I depend on you putting Miss Shaw in the Chinese bedroom and not in a less cheerful room on my account. It is scandalous to let such a pretty chamber stand idle when you entertain house guests so infrequently. I relinquish all claims to it,

*that my friend's sister might enjoy it on a more
permanent basis.
This time, I hope my recommendation proves a
long-lasting success.
I look forward to renewing my acquaintance with
Miss Shaw when we visit.
Your loving sister
Anne*

At the end of the page, there was a brief scrawl from
his brother.

*I hope you and Philip are in good health. On this
occasion, I fear Anne has overstepped the mark.
Dismiss the new governess if she does not suit. You
can trust me to deal with Anne's disappointment.
Charles*

The more John read, the more his stomach churned.
By the end of the letter, his face was flushed with the heat
of embarrassment—and guilt. He'd done nothing to
secure Miss Shaw's comfort. After putting her in Mrs
Partridge's hands, he hadn't given it another thought.

Despite knowing Miss Shaw was the sister of one of
Anne's friends. Despite seeing at a glance, she was a lady.
Despite her being unlike any of the previous governesses.

John did not even know which room Mrs Partridge
had assigned to her. Nor did he know where she took her
meals. He supposed she ate where all the other governesses
had eaten. But where was that? In the schoolroom? Good
heavens. He hoped it was not in the servants' hall with her
maid. What would Anne say if she knew?

He needed to put this right. Fast. Before Anne heard of his neglect.

John pulled on the bell rope and a footman appeared. He sent the man off to summon Mrs Partridge, who came bustling into his study.

"Please can you inform cook that from now on, Miss Shaw will take her dinner with me."

"Pardon me for speaking freely, sir, but she's a governess. She should continue dining with Philip, as all the other governesses did."

John was relieved to learn Miss Shaw had been eating in the schoolroom, not in the servants' hall, as he had feared.

"I've overlooked the fact that Miss Shaw's sister is a friend of Mrs Derringer's. In future, she will take her meals with me."

"Very good, sir," the woman said, pursing her lips in disapproval.

"And Mrs Partridge?"

"Yes, sir?"

"Which room did you allocate to Miss Shaw?"

"The same one every governess has used, next to the schoolroom."

"Please move her things to the Chinese bedchamber."

The housekeeper's face turned an alarming shade of purple. Was she trying hard not to blurt out her disapproval?

"That's all, Mrs Partridge. I expect Miss Shaw to join me in the drawing room before dinner."

The woman squeaked out something that could be interpreted as having received John's instructions and exited his study in a fluster.

John found he was chuckling to himself. Anne's letter had forced his hand, but he didn't regret the confrontation. It was a long time since he'd dared put Mrs Partridge out of countenance, but it was no bad thing to remind the woman of her place. She was too inclined to offer him advice he didn't want.

As was Miss Shaw, he reminded himself. He hoped she would not give him a daily dose of guilt with his dinner.

⸻ ❤ ⸻

EVELINA WAS WELL satisfied with her day's work. She believed she was making progress toward gaining Philip's confidence. He became more talkative as they played by the river. He had not yet shown her his secret collection of tesserae, but it was too soon for that. She did not expect it.

As they ascended the stairs, Philip chattered about their boat races and his hopes that another day they could build a dam. When they reached the top floor, Evelina shooed Philip off to the nursery to smarten up for dinner. She was about to enter her own room to do likewise when her maid hurtled up the staircase. Maggie seemed to labour under some deep emotion.

"Whatever is the matter?" Evelina asked.

The girl said nothing. Instead, she led her mistress by the hand, back the way she'd come, to the floor below. She pulled Evelina along the corridor and stopped outside a door. Pushing it open, Maggie ushered her inside.

"Look at this," she said, her eyes shining with excitement.

Evelina looked. In the middle of the large bedchamber was an elegant four-poster bed. An open doorway to the side hinted at a dressing room beyond. There was a gold-rimmed mirror over a dressing table standing between two long windows that overlooked the gardens. On the walls was an exquisite paper decorated with vibrant illustrations of Chinese bridges and rivers and all manner of exotic people and creatures.

"I think it's the most beautiful room I've ever seen," she said in an awed voice.

Maggie nodded vigorously.

Her movement brought Evelina back to her senses. "We'd better go," she said in an urgent whisper. "I'm sure we shouldn't be in here."

"That's where you'd be wrong, madam," Maggie said with glee. "Your belongings were moved here while you were outside with Master Philip—at Mr Derringer's orders. What do you say to that?"

"I...this is...unexpected." Evelina wondered what had sparked the change. She hadn't spoken to her employer in days. "Perhaps Mr Derringer recalled my sister is a friend of his brother's wife and felt my previous accommodation was unsuitable."

"I should say. This room has my full approval. That's not all. The master requests you join him for dinner."

"Mr Derringer wants to dine with me?"

"Today, and every day. Now, tell me he isn't sweet on you."

"Maggie! That's quite enough. You forget yourself. Don't just stand there, girl. Hurry. I must dress for dinner, and I don't wish to keep my employer waiting."

CHAPTER 9

*H*alf an hour later, Maggie declared her mistress was ready, and Evelina went downstairs to the drawing room. When she reached it, the butler announced her as if she were a guest. Mr Derringer stood by the window and did not turn to greet her. Evelina wondered whether he regretted the impulse that had prompted him to invite her to dine with him.

She hovered inside the doorway, fidgeting with her hands, not sure if she was free to speak, or sit, or if she should stand there until he deigned to address her. It wasn't clear if they were on an even footing or not. By asking her to dine with him, he treated her as his social equal, but as his employee she should be beneath his notice, whatever her background.

Evelina stood in silence until Mr Partridge re-entered the room and announced that dinner was served.

Mr Derringer did not move from his position by the window. Evelina wondered whether her employer was deaf. Hadn't he heard what the man said?

The butler didn't seem put out by the lack of

response. He walked half-way across the room and repeated his announcement.

Mr Derringer jerked round as if hearing his words for the first time.

"Thank you, Partridge." His eyes rested on Evelina. "Miss Shaw...I didn't hear you come in...I am so glad you could join me."

Offering her his arm as if she were a guest, they walked along the corridor to the dining room. The long rectangular table, that she reckoned seated ten or twelve, was laid with just two places, one at either end.

Mr Derringer drew his eyebrows together in a frown, but said nothing, taking her to her chair before seating himself opposite.

The arrangement was not calculated to set her at her ease. It would be hard to engage in polite conversation with the distance between them, as she would have to raise her voice to speak to Mr Derringer. And all the while, Mr Partridge lingered in the background, directing the footmen. Evelina had the distinct impression the man did not approve of her eating with his master—or did he always appear that dour?

They ate in silence—a silence which grew more oppressive the longer it continued. Evelina yearned to escape and was relieved when the cloth was removed.

After rising from the table, she walked to the door, where she paused.

"Goodnight, Mr Derringer."

He glanced up, a vacant expression in his eyes as he peered at her through his spectacles. "Are you leaving?"

She gave a weak smile. "I believe it is customary. I expect you would like a glass of port."

"Yes, of course. How stupid of me. It has been a while..."

"I bid you goodnight."

"Goodnight, Miss Shaw. I look forward to your company again tomorrow."

Evelina repressed a sigh. She couldn't repeat the experience with any enthusiasm if it was going to be this torturous.

***

JOHN WATCHED Evelina leave the room, his eyes resting on her retreating form until the door shut behind her. He was alone again. And for the first time in months, it bothered him.

Although they had exchanged few words since entering the dining room, he had found it comforting to have another person in the room besides servants.

John wondered what she must think of him, continually distracted and needing to be awakened from his perpetual stupor. Tomorrow he would do better. He would talk to her.

After staring down the length of the table, he reached a decision. He wouldn't accept this arrangement again. With a nod of his head, he summoned the butler, who stood by the sideboard where a variety of drinks awaited him.

"Partridge, does this table have leaves?"

The butler looked at him in bewilderment.

"Can you make it shorter?" John asked, attempting to explain where he was coming from.

"Yes, sir."

"Then please take the leaves out before I sit down to eat my dinner tomorrow, so I can converse with Miss Shaw without having to shout."

The butler hesitated. "Begging your pardon, sir, but I understood this was how you wanted the table. The leaves were Mrs Partridge's orders."

John hid his frustration at his housekeeper's interference and nodded. "Very proper, but quite unnecessary. No leaves tomorrow, please."

"Yes, sir."

"And now pour me a glass of that fine port you have there."

The worried expression on Mr Partridge's face vanished as he made his request—the type of request a butler expected a gentleman to make after dinner. After receiving his glass of port, John dismissed the man with the wave of a finger, leaving him alone with his thoughts.

CHAPTER 10

*E*velina didn't know what to think of Mr Derringer. Yesterday, he had installed her in a beautiful bedchamber and invited her to dine with him, but then he had spoken only half a dozen words to her while they ate. True, the length of the table had not helped, but he could have talked to her in the drawing room beforehand if he'd not been so distracted.

Or he could have asked her to join him for coffee afterward—but he hadn't. It was going to be excruciating to endure an hour of virtual silence at dinner every day. She would prefer to eat with Philip.

She mounted the stairs to the schoolroom to have breakfast with her pupil, hoping the change in their eating arrangements would not distress him.

To her surprise, he wasn't there. Nor was there any sign of Polly or their meal.

Evelina wondered if she had made a mistake. Was she supposed to eat her breakfast with Mr Derringer, as well as dinner? But what of Philip? Where was the boy?

She knocked on the door of his bedchamber, and his nurse appeared.

"Is Philip there?"

"Goodness, no. He's with his uncle."

"With his uncle?"

"Yes, Miss Shaw. It's Wednesday. They've gone to Bath. Didn't you know?"

"Yes, of course," Evelina said, remembering what Mrs Partridge had told her. On Wednesdays, Mr Derringer took Philip to visit his parents. "I forgot. What time do they normally return?"

"Not until after dinner," the woman assured her. "You've got the whole day to yourself."

Evelina digested the information as she walked back downstairs. She would not be dining with Mr Derringer tonight, as he had intimated. He must have forgotten what day of the week it was. That would not surprise her.

When she reached her room, a welcome sight greeted her. Maggie had just finished laying out some breakfast things on the table. "Polly brought you up a tray. Shall I pour you some tea?"

"No, I'll pour my own. Now, off you go to the servants' hall for your own meal, Maggie."

Her maid bobbed a curtsey, and hurried away, leaving Evelina alone.

A break from teaching should have been pleasant, but without her pupil, her day lacked purpose. She put on her half-boots and pelisse and spent the morning trudging through the grounds, before wiling away the afternoon, curled up on her bed with a book. By dinnertime, she had endured as much of her own company as she cared for, and she thought even the dour presence of Mr Partridge would be a welcome relief.

With Mr Derringer away, there was no need to dress for dinner, but Evelina could not reconcile herself to make no change in her appearance. The practice was ingrained in her. She'd dressed for dinner ever since entering society some six years earlier. She asked Maggie to tidy her hair and picked up her Norwich shawl to drape over her shoulders in place of the Spencer jacket she had worn all day.

As she looked in the mirror before making her way downstairs, she wondered who she was trying to impress. Not Mr Partridge, she thought with a laugh. Or was she? Maybe she wanted to impress him—just a little. To dress for dinner set her apart from the servants—a distinction she was keen to emphasise, even more so with Mr Derringer absent.

Before she could see if her appearance impressed Mr Partridge, there was a knock on the door. Her maid opened it to reveal Polly laden down with a tray of food.

"Where would you like me to put it, madam?" she asked.

Maggie cleared the occasional table so Polly could put the tray down.

"It is kind of you to bring me a tray, but I did not expect to eat in my room."

Polly bit her lip. "I'm sorry if it's not what you were expecting, Miss Shaw, but Mrs Partridge said as how you wouldn't be eating in the dining room with the master away, and she gave me this tray to bring up to you, so I thought..."

Evelina hastened to reassure the flustered maid. "Please don't fret, Polly. This will be more comfortable than eating in solitary state."

Having spread the dishes on the table, Polly bobbed a

curtsey and fled. It was not until after she had gone that Evelina realised she had nothing to drink. She asked Maggie to ring the bell, and began her meal, filling her plate from the dishes Polly had brought.

By the time Evelina had finished eating, she was feeling put out. The bell remained unanswered, despite Maggie ringing a second time, and Polly had not come back with a dessert course.

Evelina's spirits sank. Mrs Partridge had been unfriendly toward her from the start, and she wondered if Mr Derringer's favour had made the housekeeper even more resentful of her presence. Having her bell ignored made her wonder if the lack of wine was deliberate, and not a careless omission. Though she did not relish taking on Mrs Partridge with Mr Derringer absent, she could not ignore such neglect.

She abandoned the half-empty dishes, which she hoped Polly would, at some point, return to collect, and descended the two flights of stairs to the basement and started along the corridor to the kitchen.

As she passed Mrs Partridge's door, she heard raised voices coming from inside the room. The housekeeper and her morose husband, the butler, she assumed. Mrs Partridge's voice grew louder. Evelina could not help hearing every word.

"It's too late for that," the woman snarled. "You wouldn't still be here if it wasn't for me."

Evelina shuddered. She had not warmed to the butler, but if that was how Mrs Partridge talked to her husband, she had some sympathy for him. The woman was a bully. Was that why the butler always looked so miserable?

"But I don't understand," a voice cried in anguish. "I thought you were helping me. What am I going to do?"

"Stop wailing, Father. You're going to keep your mouth shut and do as I say," Mrs Partridge said.

The voices dropped, and Evelina heard no more. Not that she wanted to. It was bad enough when she believed Mrs Partridge was talking to her husband and had reduced him to a state where he would whine like that. For a woman to talk to her father with such a lack of respect was...disgraceful.

She hurried down the corridor to the kitchen, and the cook bustled over to the entrance, wiping her hands on her apron.

"Is anything wrong, Miss Shaw? I hope you enjoyed your dinner."

"I did, Mrs Coombes, but—"

"Yes?"

"I didn't expect you to go to the same trouble as when Mr Derringer is dining at home, but—"

The cook's face took on an alarming hue. "I would be ashamed to lower my standards when Mr Derringer is absent. Whatever Mrs Partridge says, I can see you are a lady—which she most assuredly is not—and I am most put out that you found the meal lacking."

Evelina saw she had ruffled the cook's feathers and hastened to reassure her. "Everything was delicious. The only thing lacking was dessert. I confess to liking sweet things and was a bit disappointed, but it does me good to go without now and then."

"No dessert? But I baked you an apple pie."

"How strange. There was no apple pie."

"I don't understand, Miss Shaw. Never say the maid

didn't bring it up? It was on the second tray with a plate of macaroons."

The cook called Polly over. "What happened to Miss Shaw's pie? Did you take a fancy to it, my girl?"

Polly looked flustered. "I never touched anything on the tray, Mrs Coombes. I swear I didn't."

"Wait a minute—how many trays did you take up?"

"One. That's all I was given."

"That explains it then," said Evelina, glad to have the mystery solved. "No doubt the wine was on the second tray with the pie."

"Let's find out what happened to it," said Mrs Coombes, marching along the corridor to the housekeeper's room before Evelina could object. The cook knocked on the door, and then retired to a respectful distance behind Evelina.

The door was flung open, and Mr Partridge filled the doorway, a sour expression on his face. His normally refined accent was absent. "What d'you want?"

Intimidated by his forbidding form, Evelina took a step back, but not before she'd caught a whiff of spirits on the butler's breath. Her sympathy for him as a browbeaten husband evaporated. She disapproved of him drinking at this time of day and feared he and his wife were taking advantage of Mr Derringer's absence.

"I would like a word with Mrs Partridge," Evelina said before her courage ran out.

"You can't. She's eating and—"

Before he finished his sentence, Evelina heard Mrs Partridge's voice from within the room.

"Who is it?"

"Miss Shaw," the butler called over his shoulder.

Evelina heard a chair being scraped along the floor

and Mr Partridge fell back so his wife could take his place in the doorway. She had a napkin in her hand and wiped what looked like a piece of pastry from her lips before she spoke.

"Forgive my husband, Miss Shaw," she said in a silky tone that did not match the look of disapproval on her face. "He knows I dislike being disturbed at dinnertime. But seeing as I *have* been disturbed, what can I do for you?"

Evelina took a deep breath, refusing to be cowed by Mrs Partridge's unhelpful attitude.

"I believe there has been a mistake," Evelina said. "Mrs Coombes said she prepared an apple pie for my dinner, but no pie was brought up to my room. Nor, might I add, was there any wine to drink with my meal."

Mrs Partridge cast a look of loathing in the cook's direction and then fixed her hawk-like eyes on Evelina.

"Dear me," she said. "Thank you for bringing this to my attention. I would not have thought it of Polly."

"I'm certain Polly is not to blame," said Evelina, eager to protect the maid.

"She says she brought up everything you gave her," Mrs Coombes added.

"A likely story. I will have to dismiss her. It wouldn't do for the servants to get fat on your dinner now, would it, Miss Shaw?"

Mrs Partridge had backed her into a corner. For Polly's sake, Evelina did not dare to pursue the issue any further. "It is no matter. I'm sure it was an oversight. Please think nothing more of it."

"Very good, miss," said Mrs Partridge, shutting the door in her face.

"Wait here," Mrs Coombes said to Evelina.

The cook bustled down the corridor and, a few minutes later, returned with a tray containing tea things and a plate of macaroons.

"We both know what became of my pie," she said with a sniff, casting a scornful glance at Mrs Partridge's door, "but there's nought I can do about it. I can, however, give you a nice cup of tea and a bite of something sweet."

"Thank you," Evelina said, taking the tray. It was reassuring to know she possessed some friends below stairs. Mrs Partridge was not one of them. And to judge from the woman's treatment of her own father, she was a formidable opponent.

CHAPTER 11

The next morning, Evelina took her breakfast with Philip in the schoolroom, as usual. She feared she might have lost some ground in gaining his confidence by not seeing him for a day, but she need not have worried. As they ate, Philip told her all about his trip to Bath and how they wouldn't be going again for weeks, as his grandparents were leaving to visit Weymouth.

After a morning studying the history of England, they went outside to build a dam across the narrowest part of the stream. Evelina allowed Philip to take off his shoes and socks and paddle in the water as he piled up stones to alter the course of the river. It was a warm day, and Evelina longed to join him, but she resisted the temptation. She helped him as best she could from the water's edge.

All was well until Philip slipped and fell in, and Evelina had to take a soggy boy back to the house. While she was instructing a maid to fetch some towels, Mrs Partridge appeared, a scowl on her face. It was as if she had been ready to pounce on them as soon as they entered the house.

"You're a disgrace, Master Philip," she said. "Mr Derringer doesn't pay the servants to clean the floor so you can make muddy puddles all over it."

"It's only a drop of water, Mrs Partridge," Evelina said, coming alongside Philip.

"Try telling that to the maids who'll have to redo the entire floor."

Evelina glared at the woman. "Bring me a mop and I'll clean up the mess myself."

"Oh no. Mr Derringer wouldn't like that. Even your maid is above cleaning floors."

Though Mrs Partridge's words could be deemed respectful, her tone was derisive, and Evelina coloured up under the housekeeper's uncompromising stare.

"Thank you, Polly," Evelina said with relief as the maid came along the corridor with two fluffy white towels in her arms. The relief was short-lived when she realised Philip had disappeared while she had been trying to pacify the housekeeper. She was certain where she would find him.

"You need not worry, Mrs Partridge. I will ensure Philip is dry before I bring him back inside." She hurried out the door in the direction of the stables, hoping the woman would not follow her.

As expected, Philip was in a tussle with the stable boy again.

"Stop this at once," Evelina said, pulling the boys apart. The stable boy ran off, leaving Philip standing there alone, hanging his head so low it rested on his chest.

"Fighting is no way to deal with your anger," Evelina

said, as she wrapped one towel around his shoulders and rubbed him down with the other, and led him back to the house.

"But Mrs Partridge—"

"No buts, Philip. You need to control yourself. You can't lash out every time someone upsets you."

The boy muttered under his breath all the way upstairs to his room, where Evelina handed him over to the care of a maidservant.

She hoped Philip had listened to her. Her heart went out to the hurting boy, struggling to deal with his emotions, but she knew he must learn to keep his temper in check before it landed him in worse trouble. She was only the governess, not his mother. She would not always be there to rescue him.

———— • ————

WHEN THE DINNER HOUR ARRIVED, John found Miss Shaw waiting for him in the drawing room. He offered her his arm and together they went in to dine.

He was glad to see Partridge had followed his orders and removed the leaves of the table, making it much more suitable for two.

It was clear from the look on Miss Shaw's face that the change in their seating arrangements surprised her.

"I thought it might make it easier to hold a conversation," he said.

"I'm certain it will."

Neither of them spoke again until after the first course had been served. At his request, the butler and footman then withdrew.

"I trust you enjoyed your day off yesterday, Miss Shaw."

"Thank you. I did."

"What did you do?"

"I spent the morning outside, exploring the grounds. Then I curled up with a book in the exquisite room you've given me. I haven't thanked you sufficiently for it, Mr Derringer. Even my maid is impressed."

"I am happy for it."

John fell silent and applied himself to his dinner, not knowing what else to say. It was as if he had forgotten the art of conversation.

"I'm sure you would like to learn how your nephew is progressing."

Miss Shaw's tone was firm. It was not a question. She assumed he was disinterested, but she was going to tell him whether or not he wanted to hear.

John nodded. It was what Miss Shaw wanted.

"For the most part, his progress is excellent.

"For the most part?"

"I am afraid Philip is yet to master his temper. When he gets angry, he picks a fight with the stable boy. But he is paying more attention to his studies now. I have discovered he is fond of the stream, and we spend some of each afternoon by the water. It serves as a powerful incentive for learning his lessons."

"Might I ask what you studied today?" John said, keen to show some interest in the boy's education.

"History. Philip can't recite the kings of England yet, but he told me many facts about the Romans. Have you been teaching him yourself?"

John stiffened. "His father shared my love of classical antiquities. He must have talked about it with his son."

"I see. As your nephew is so interested in that period of history, perhaps you could share your knowledge with him as your brother once did."

"I...I..." His voice trailed off. It was a reasonable suggestion, but the idea of filling in for his brother made John feel nauseous. "My work is too complex for a child to understand. Maybe when he is older..."

Miss Shaw looked disappointed, but John would not change his mind. He could not take Robert's place in Philip's life. Not now. Not ever.

DURING THE FOLLOWING WEEKS, John noticed a new peace settling over his household, and with it, a sense of contentment he had not experienced in a long time. Though he dared not admit it, even to himself, he suspected it had something to do with Miss Shaw.

If he were honest, it had quite a lot to do with Miss Shaw. Despite the way she continued to prod his conscience over his lack of involvement in Philip's life.

John continued to spend several hours each day cataloguing his collections and dealing with estate business. Miss Shaw continued to teach Philip and, judging by the lack of interruptions he had to face, his nephew's behaviour was improving.

And every day she dined with John.

He often found the second half of the afternoon dragged, and today was no exception. He looked at his pocket watch to check the hour. Five o'clock. A half-smile crept onto his lips. Nearly time to change his dress and go to the drawing room.

When had dinnertime with Miss Shaw become the climax of his day? Seeing her every evening gave him something to look forward to. He had become so accustomed to solitude since moving back to Duriel Hall he had not realised how lonely he had become. Now he was comfortable with her presence at the table, he no longer felt alone. He wondered how he had coped before Miss Shaw had arrived.

Once the first course was served, John began the conversation in the same way he began it every time.

"Tell me about your day, Miss Shaw. What have you been teaching my nephew?"

"The most tedious of subjects—Latin verbs."

"You have learned Latin? You continue to amaze me."

"I am astonished you hired me to teach Philip if you weren't aware of my accomplishments. My knowledge of Latin is, I confess, rudimentary. I only learned enough to teach my sister's stepsons so they would be ready for Eton."

"And how did he behave? No fighting today, I hope."

"You should have more faith in Philip. He hasn't resorted to fighting for three weeks."

"That's good news. And no locking you in the schoolroom?"

"No indeed. He has not tried that one again."

"I am relieved to hear it."

"Yes. Philip's behaviour has continued to improve. Your nephew is a delightful child," she added, fixing him with a meaningful stare.

John wriggled in his seat. Not a day went by without Miss Shaw plucking at the strings of his conscience. It pleased him the boy was making progress—really, it did.

But why must she make it personal—always reminding him Philip was his nephew?

He shuddered as he remembered how their second dinner together had ended when he had shied away from sharing his work with the boy. Miss Shaw had looked so disappointed. John had shown an interest in Philip's progress ever since, trying to restore her faith in him, but he feared she wanted him to give more to his nephew than he could.

"While the weather remains fine, we're continuing to spend most afternoons down by the river," Miss Shaw said, filling the silence. "Today, we practised engineering, trying to build a bridge from one side to the other with some planks of wood your groundsman gave us. Perhaps—"

She broke off and eyed John uncertainly. "Perhaps you would like to join us one afternoon."

His chest tightened with anxiety as her words sank in. There she was, doing it again. Always hinting he should be more involved with his nephew. But he could not. How could he replace his brother in Philip's life? If he tried, he would fail. It was better for Philip—better for everyone—if he didn't try.

But Miss Shaw's gentle suggestion pierced the wall John had built around himself—the wall that protected him from failing. If he backed off and rebuilt the wall, he would disappoint her again. And the fear of disappointing Miss Shaw was now as great as the fear of failing.

He took a deep breath. "Perhaps."

CHAPTER 12

*M*r Derringer's words inspired Evelina with hope—hope that he would build a relationship with his nephew. But five days passed, and Mr Derringer did not join them down by the river or even come up to the schoolroom. Evelina feared she had placed too much weight on the word 'perhaps'.

It wasn't the only concern pressing on her mind. She had not forgotten about the tesserae she had found hidden under the bridge. She had hoped Philip would show her his treasures of his own free will. But though he now spoke openly with her, he did not take her to his secret hiding place. The longer he went without showing her, the more she feared he had stolen the pieces of Roman mosaic from his uncle's study.

As they went outside that afternoon, Evelina suggested they did something different.

"Do you like blackberries?" she asked.

Philip nodded.

"Do you know what time of year we pick them to eat?"

His eyes grew wide. "Now?"

"The start of August is quite early for blackberries, but we've had a lot of sunshine over the last few weeks and while we were down at the stream yesterday, I spotted a bush with some ripe fruit on it. Shall we look for some?"

"Can we eat them?"

Evelina laughed. "That depends on how many we find. You could ask Mrs Partridge for a basket to put them in."

Philip screwed up his face. "Do I have to?"

"You will spoil your jacket if you fill your pockets with them."

"I don't want to go to Mrs Partridge. She hates me."

Evelina sympathised with Philip's sentiments, but she knew it was her duty not to foster such a violent reaction in her pupil.

"I'm sure she does not."

"Yes, she does. She keeps saying I should be sent away to school and won't let me see my uncle."

"Hmm. You haven't helped yourself there in the past, have you?"

Philip hung his head. "I thought that if..."

"Yes?"

"Nothing."

With sagging shoulders, he disappeared into the house and came back with a small basket. His face was beaming.

"Mrs Partridge wasn't there, so cook gave me one of her baskets."

They headed toward the stream and stopped on the other side of the bridge, where there were several enormous horse chestnut trees. Evelina found a wall to perch on and sat, enjoying a few rare moments of peace as Philip explored the bush she had discovered, filling his basket with blackberries—those that didn't make their way into his mouth.

Evelina absentmindedly ran her hands over the wall where she was perched. She wondered what it belonged to. It was high enough to sit on, but had sunk into the ground and been much higher in the past. It looked older than the bridge, but how much older she didn't know. She called Philip over to see. It would be an excellent exercise for him to learn by observation.

He was not pleased to have his activity interrupted, but they had reached a sufficient understanding that he did not refuse.

"Look at this wall on which I'm sitting. Why do you think it's here?"

Philip scratched his head. "People sometimes have walls around their estates, but this isn't the edge of our land, and it wouldn't be much good for that anyway—it isn't long enough and it's not very tall either."

He ran his palms along the wall as Evelina had done, but kept going until he reached the end of the section. Crouching down, he scooped a mound of earth aside with his hands, and then another. As he cleared the rest away, he jumped up with excitement.

"Look—there's more, but it's fallen down."

"So there is. Does that change your mind about why the wall is here? What else might it be?"

"It could be a building," Philip said after a few moments' reflection, "but it doesn't seem likely. Why would anyone build a house so near the river?"

"Perhaps the water wasn't here when they built it."

Philip screwed up his forehead in confusion. "I don't understand. How can the wall be older than the river?"

"I expect the stream was somewhere nearby—but not right here. A river can change its course over time, depending on the flow of the water and the sort of ground it is passing through."

Philip paid attention to her words and then pondered them in silence. At length, his eyes lit up.

"Do you...do you think the wall could be Roman?"

"I don't know..."

"Stay here," he said, holding up his hand toward her.

He scampered down the river bank and along the side of the stream until he reached the bridge. Evelina remained where she was. She wondered if he was going to fetch his collection of tesserae.

A few minutes later, he climbed up the bank again, his trousers much dirtier than they had been before.

"Hold out your hands."

As Evelina obeyed, he dropped the small collection of red, light brown and white tesserae into her palms.

"Oh," she exclaimed, as if she had not seen them before. "What have we got here?"

"They are Roman tesserae," he said, a touch of pride in his voice. "Father and Uncle John used to visit places where they were digging up old buildings and sometimes people sold bits to them."

"Are these from your uncle's collection?" Evelina asked, holding her breath while she waited for him to answer.

Philip scowled. "Of course not. I'm not allowed anywhere near Uncle John's collections. These are mine. I found them."

Evelina could breathe again. Philip was not a thief.

"Where did you find them?"

"I'll show you."

Philip clambered down the bank again, not by the bridge, but below where they were standing, near to the wall.

Evelina followed, casting a wary eye at the river, which was swollen because of the heavy rain the previous night. She hoped she would not slip.

Philip crouched down by the side of the water and turned over the pebbles in front of him.

"I found them about here," he said. "Not at once, but over several days. I haven't had the chance to search for more—not since you came."

He shot her a cheeky grin. "It's not so easy to get away from you—not that I want to," he added when Evelina raised her eyebrows. "Not now."

"Why didn't you show me before?" she asked. "Didn't you think I'd be interested?"

Philip's head drooped. "I thought the tesserae would interest Uncle John, but Mrs Partridge wouldn't let me show him."

"I'm sorry. I expect it was an inconvenient time. Your uncle would be fascinated if he knew."

He looked up, a glimmer of hope in his eyes. "Do you really think so?"

Evelina nodded and gave him a reassuring smile. She hoped she was right. Her heart ached to witness Philip's insecurity. It was tragic he felt so unsure of his uncle's regard. Not after losing his parents.

"I will come with you, Philip, and we can show your uncle your finds together. Would you like that?"

The boy nodded vigorously.

"Ten more minutes and we'll go in and show him before you go up for your dinner."

Philip spent the remaining time splashing around in the water, moving the stones about, hoping to find more tesserae.

"I found one," he cried, holding up another small cube of red stone. "How many have I got now?"

Evelina held out her palms so Philip could count the pieces of mosaic.

"Twelve!" he said with delight. He eyed the basket, biting his lip in concentration. "It would be easier to carry the tesserae if I put them in here, but some of the berries are a bit oozy, and I don't want to risk staining the pieces with blackberry juice. I think I'll make a nest for them."

Philip set to work, pulling up long stalks of grass, and laying them on top of the blackberries at one end of the basket. Evelina helped him craft them into a cocoon, ready to receive his collection of tesserae.

"I wish I could figure out how they fit together," he said as they made their way back to the house, "but I don't suppose I shall ever know what pattern they make."

"Your uncle might be able to help. Maybe he has seen a design using these colours before."

"Oh, yes. Perhaps he has."

It was with difficulty that Evelina restrained Philip from running along the corridor to his uncle's study and bursting into the room unannounced.

He hopped from one foot to another in impatience, dripping onto the floor as he did so, as Evelina knocked on the door.

Mr Derringer called to them to enter, and Evelina ushered Philip into the study in front of her.

The expression on her employer's face was not encouraging. His gaze flitted from her to Philip and back again, with what she could only describe as a scowl.

"Pray, excuse us for disturbing you, Mr Derringer, but Philip has something to show you."

"Yes?" he barked.

Evelina could see Philip's courage failing. Bother the man. Why couldn't he make more effort with his own nephew? She gave Philip a gentle push on the small of his back.

"I found these and thought you'd like to see them, Uncle John. You may keep them, if you want."

He placed the basket on the desk and stepped back, his blue eyes mirroring his insecurity as he watched his uncle, waiting to find out how he reacted.

Evelina held her breath as she, too, waited.

Mr Derringer gave a fleeting glance at the wicker container and then glared at his nephew. "Get that off my desk at once."

The boy snatched his precious basket back and stood there, his bottom lip quivering.

His uncle didn't seem to notice the effect his words had on Philip. He was too busy staring in disgust at the reddish splodge in front of him. "Look at the mess you've made."

Mr Derringer shifted his gaze to observe the puddle forming at Philip's feet and then turned his glare on Evelina. "What were you thinking of, Miss Shaw, bringing my nephew in here in this state? He's dripping all over the floor. Take him away and get him cleaned up. Now."

Evelina's heart sank. This interview had not worked out as she hoped.

"I told you he wouldn't be interested," Philip said, almost snarling at Evelina.

"That is no way to address your governess, boy."

"Why should you care? You don't care about anything else I do," Philip said, his voice rising as he spat out his words at his uncle. "Why don't you send me to school and then you won't ever have to look at me again? You don't want me. No one wants me anymore."

Basket in hand, he raced out the door, slamming it behind him.

Evelina took a few deep breaths, trying to calm her racing heart. Her lips curled downward in contempt as she stared in disbelief at Mr Derringer, who looked shocked at his nephew's outburst.

She had run out of sympathy for her employer. How dare he treat his nephew like that? It was not Philip's fault he had been foisted upon an uncle who didn't want him. An uncle with no experience of children who seemed not the slightest bit interested in learning how to relate to his nephew.

But Philip *was* Mr Derringer's responsibility, whether or not he liked it. However unwelcome that responsibility was, it did not justify such callous behaviour, and Evelina had every intention of telling him so. She hoped she would still be Philip's governess at the end of it.

CHAPTER 13

*J*ohn's mouth fell open in amazement as he gaped at the door Philip had just slammed. What had just happened? He had never seen his nephew lose his temper like that before.

His gaze drifted to the woman who stood in front of him, who stared at him as if he were an ogre with three heads. A keen sense of ill use ousted the shock of Philip's angry outburst. The incident would not have occurred if Miss Shaw had not brought his nephew into his study in that bedraggled state. It was her fault, not his, and yet she stood there, accusing him with her eyes, as if she thought the opposite.

"What?" John snapped as Miss Shaw continued to glare at him.

She shook her head slowly from side to side, despair —no, contempt—written all over her face. John found her gaze uncomfortable and looked away.

"The boy was putting water everywhere," he said. His voice sounded sulky even in his own ears.

"That *boy* is your nephew, Mr Derringer. Couldn't

you put your scruples aside for a few minutes to see what he was so excited about? Did you look at what he was showing you before dismissing it so heartlessly?"

"Of course, I did. A grand collection of blackberries. He couldn't think it worth disturbing me for that."

"Disturbing you? Is that what Philip is?" she asked. "A disturbance?"

Miss Shaw's voice pierced his innermost being, although she did not raise her volume.

He could sense her eyes boring into him, even though he refused to meet her gaze. "I never wanted children." He was so used to saying the words, he almost believed them.

Deep down, he knew it wasn't true, but it was easier to stick with the lie—that this was the path he had chosen. The alternative was too unpleasant to contemplate. "If I had wanted children, I would have married and had my own."

"I'm relieved you've saved some poor female from marriage if the only reason you would take a wife is to beget an heir. That is almost as bad as marrying to get a mother for your children."

John cringed when he heard the rancour in her voice and remembered their first conversation—how she had dismissed such a marriage for herself. He did not care for the comparison.

Her words goaded him to defend himself. "That is not the only reason I would marry. I observed the love that Robert had for Sarah—the friendship, the companionship they shared—and decided I could settle for nothing less. Alas, I don't have my brother's charm," he said in a voice tinged with regret, "and never found a woman who wanted to be my friend."

John broke off, horrified at what he had revealed. What was it about Miss Shaw that tore down his defences? He couldn't bear the thought of seeing pity in her eyes and kept his head down as he continued.

"Don't feel sorry for me. Save all your compassion for Philip. He has been saddled with a wretched excuse of an uncle instead of his father. It should be Robert here, looking after Philip, not me. Why did he have to die...?"

"You miss him, don't you?" she whispered.

John blinked away the moisture that had gathered unbidden in his eyes. There she was, doing it again. Piercing his defences. Of course, he missed Robert. He was his brother—and his best friend.

"It is a challenge we face in this life," she whispered. "The deeper we love, the more deeply it hurts when that love ends."

John risked a glance at Miss Shaw and noticed the contempt had vanished and only tenderness remained.

"Don't you understand?" she said. "Philip's parents loved him, and now they're gone. That love is missing from his life. He's broken, and he's looking to you now. You have the power to make him feel loved again."

John turned away. What Miss Shaw was asking was hard. Too hard. He couldn't be a father to Philip. He could never replace Robert in the boy's life.

"I don't know how to deal with children."

"And yet, Philip holds you in great esteem—at least, he did until today."

That gave John pause for thought.

"Did you spend no time with your nephew when your brother was alive?"

John allowed himself to remember what he had buried in the back of his mind. "Philip sometimes used to tag along with Robert and I when we went to examine the latest reports of a Roman find. We would have liked to travel to Pompeii and Herculaneum, but the war against Napoleon made it impossible. I've studied all Mr Westlake's papers on the subject, and the detailed drawings in his and other works have enabled me to identify as Roman what other people saw as rubble. We got quite a name for ourselves amongst the antiquarian community, and many people would write to us, inviting us to investigate what they had found whilst excavating foundations for a new house, hoping that they would have something we would buy from them."

"Philip has inherited his father's love for Roman artifacts—a love that you share."

John screwed up his face. "But he didn't...he couldn't..." He paused. "He's only a boy."

"He may be only a boy, but he is far from stupid, Mr Derringer. If you treat him like a piece of unwanted furniture, he will soon believe that is who he is. Is that how you view him? As an unwelcome inheritance?"

John squirmed at her words. What was it about this woman that she dared to ask such impertinent questions—questions that pierced through his carefully constructed armour and made him vulnerable?

"I didn't mean to make the boy feel unwanted..."

"Philip. His name is Philip. If you referred to him more by his name than by such a cold term as 'boy', you would view him more as a person than as an object."

Heat suffused John's cheeks. Is that how she thought he saw his nephew?

"Do you know what Philip offered you?"

"His prize collection of blackberries?" he said in a sarcastic voice.

"Even if that was all he offered, it would have been kinder to accept the gift with at least the semblance of pleasure. But no. He presented you with much more, and you didn't even take the time to examine his offering."

John's confusion must have shown on his face, as Miss Shaw continued with no response from him.

"Philip did offer you his prize collection, but not of blackberries—of his precious Roman tesserae."

"You must be mistaken, Miss Shaw. Philip has no such collection."

"Do you know that for certain?"

"Are you saying my brother gave him some Roman finds of his own?"

She shook her head. "No. It is his collection, because he found them. On your land."

Now John's interest was genuine. "On my land? Where? You must show me. I had no idea—"

"I'm afraid not. The discovery was Philip's, not mine." She fixed him with another piercing stare, coaxing him with her words.

"If you want to see his tesserae and where he found them, you must make your peace with your nephew. You must apologise for your harsh words."

"You wish me to apologise to my nephew—a mere boy? Are you out of your mind?"

The warmth in Miss Shaw's expression vanished. "If we have wronged another, we must ask for forgiveness. I am not aware that Scripture places any age restrictions on the process."

John picked up a cloth and dabbed at the damp patch on his desk which the basket had left. He needed to give his hands something to do, and it gave his eyes a new direction, away from Miss Shaw's penetrating gaze.

"You don't know what you are asking. Philip will never respect me again if I show such weakness as to admit that I was in the wrong."

Miss Shaw had the audacity to laugh at him. "How differently we view our mistakes, Mr Derringer. You believe Philip will cease to respect you if you apologise, whereas I see it as both necessary and desirable. Not only would you be demonstrating the way to restore relationships with those closest to you, but you would also reveal your own vulnerability. That you, too, are imperfect."

"You believe that is a good thing?" John couldn't keep the scepticism out of his voice.

"Yes. Now, I will do my part, Mr Derringer. I will try to bring Philip to realise that it was wrong of him to shout at you. But if I bring him to your study to apologise, can I rely on you to respond in kind? If you do not, I despair of you ever having a good relationship with your nephew."

"Those are harsh words, Miss Shaw."

"You have hurt Philip deeply. If you don't take steps to make him feel wanted, he will carry it with him for the rest of his life."

John let out a deep sigh. "Very well. I will try. But please stop the boy—" He hastily changed his words when Miss Shaw scowled at him. "Please stop *Philip* dripping before you bring him back."

She smiled at him as if he were a small boy needing encouragement. "I promise."

CHAPTER 14

$\mathcal{E}$velina climbed the stairs to the schoolroom. She didn't expect to find Philip there, but she had to check before she searched elsewhere.

She trusted the damage done to his self-worth was not irreparable, and that, having persuaded Mr Derringer to play his part in the apology, Philip would admit he had erred too.

As expected, the schoolroom was empty. Oh dear. She hoped he was not taking out his frustration on the stable boy. It would be regrettable if Mrs Partridge took him to his uncle's study in disgrace again.

She hurried outside to the stables. The housekeeper was ahead of her. She rushed to catch her up, and it was fortunate she did. The sight that met her eyes as she walked into the yard confirmed her fears. Philip was lying on top of the stable lad, who was rolling around on the cobbles, trying to escape the bigger boy's hold.

Mrs Partridge called out to the chief groom, but before the man responded, Evelina stepped forward.

"Please do not let Philip take up anymore of your precious time, Mrs Partridge. I can handle this."

The housekeeper gave her a haughty glare, turned on her heel, and returned to the house. Evelina heaved a sigh of relief and faced her charge and his opponent.

"Break it up. At once."

Philip was momentarily distracted, and the other boy thrust him away so roughly he banged his head on the ground. The stable lad looked scared and, at a nod from Evelina, he scampered off.

Philip sat up and rubbed the back of his skull. Evelina offered him a hand, but he refused to take it, scrambling to his feet without her aid.

She grabbed him by the arm and marched him out of the yard and back toward the house.

"To pick a fight is a poor way to deal with your troubles."

Philip scowled at her.

"Also, it wasn't fair to your opponent, as he is not the person you are angry with."

Philip kicked up some stones with his foot, sending a shower of pebbles into the air.

"I find it best to face up to my problems, rather than run away from them, otherwise they grow into something too big for me to handle. Do you know what I'm talking about?"

He gave a brief nod. It was not encouraging, but at least it showed he was listening.

Evelina took him up to his bedroom and rang for a servant to draw him a bath.

"When you are clean and dressed in dry clothes, we will talk. Come to the schoolroom when you're ready."

She sat and waited, hoping Philip would come of his

own volition and she would not have to go in search of him again. Three quarters of an hour later, he appeared at the door, a semi-contrite expression on his face.

Evelina beckoned him in, and he stood before her, his head drooped so low that his chin almost touched his chest.

"I'm sorry to have disappointed you, Miss Shaw."

"Apology accepted," said Evelina, "but the offence was not against me, was it?"

Philip shook his head. "I've already prayed to God and said I was sorry, but I don't know whether he will forgive me."

Evelina put a finger under his chin and lifted it until Philip was forced to look into her eyes.

"God always forgives us if we're truly sorry."

"I don't think he loves me."

"Of course, God loves you."

"But if he loves me, why did Father and Mother die?"

Evelina sought for the right words. How could she explain why there was suffering in the world when it was such a mystery to her? She sat down and encouraged Philip to sit next to her.

He sat with his hands in his lap, waiting for her to say more. She reached out and covered his hands with her own. "It is hard to understand why bad things happen, but they do. It is part of life. I can't tell you why your parents died, but I can assure you, without the shadow of a doubt, God loves you."

Evelina let her words sink in. "Do you believe that?"

A smile spread over Philip's face.

"Now, you know there's someone else you need to apologise to."

His smile vanished. "Do I have to?"

"What did I say about facing up to your problems? You must apologise for your rudeness at some point, or your uncle will believe you are an ill-mannered boy. Do you really want him to send you to school now?"

Philip shook his head. "That's what Mrs Partridge wants, but I want to stay here with you."

"And your uncle?"

The pained look returned to his face. "I suppose. But I don't think he likes me anymore. He has no time for me."

"Maybe that will change, if you show him you are mature enough to apologise when you know you were in the wrong."

"It won't make any difference, but I'll do it for you."

"Ready?" she asked him, rising from her chair.

In answer, he stood up beside her and slipped his hand into hers.

Together, they walked down two flights of stairs and made their way to Mr Derringer's study.

He glanced up at her and when she shot him a reassuring smile, he rapped on the door.

"Enter," Mr Derringer's voice called from within.

Evelina hoped her employer would play his part, or all her work encouraging Philip to face his uncle would be wasted.

Mr Derringer rose from his chair, his jawline rigid, as though he were working hard to keep his emotions in check. He walked around to the side of the desk facing them, and perched there in a more informal manner than Evelina had witnessed before.

"I owe you an apology, Philip," Mr Derringer said before his nephew could utter a word. "I'm sorry I did not give you my full attention, but let myself get distracted by a bit of mud and water. Please forgive me for the harsh words I spoke."

"I...I'm sorry too, sir. I should not have yelled at you."

Mr Derringer held out his right hand. "Shall we shake on it? Can we be friends?"

Philip's eyes glowed with pleasure as he reached out his hand to take his uncle's outstretched one. "Yes, sir. I'd like that."

Evelina raised her eyes to meet Mr Derringer's and mouthed the words, "Thank you."

By the slightest inclination of his head, she knew he had understood her, and the warmth in his gaze suggested he was receiving as much pleasure from the reconciliation as she was.

"Now, what was it you were trying to show me, Philip?"

"Some Roman tesserae I found."

"What makes you think they are Roman tesserae?"

Philip tilted his head to one side as he thought. "They remind me of the pieces of mosaic you and Father found on the Backshall estate."

"You remember that?"

"Yes, sir. I hope you can check your books for a pattern that matches the colours I found."

"What colours did you find? Can you fetch them to show me now?"

Philip glanced at Evelina. "May I?"

"Of course you may. I suggest you wrap them in a clean handkerchief before you bring them down here— or perhaps your uncle can give you a container to put them in. The basket has made one too many appearances in your uncle's study today."

"What a good idea," Mr Derringer said. He walked to the shelves behind his desk and extracted a small cardboard box, which he handed to Philip.

"Be quick," he said. "We haven't got long before dinner."

Philip needed no further encouragement. He opened the door and ran off down the corridor, clutching the box.

"That went smoothly," Evelina said.

"To confess my error was easier than I expected and worth the embarrassment for the results it achieved. I thought Philip's eyes would pop out of their sockets when I held out my hand to him."

"It was a clever idea."

"I hadn't planned it at all. It just...happened. For a moment, he looked so like Robert that I acted as if he *were* Robert. We always shook hands after an argument. It was a way of sealing the past, I guess."

Philip soon returned with the box containing his collection of tesserae. His uncle invited him to come and stand next to his chair while they examined his Roman treasures together.

Evelina watched, marvelling at the transformation in her employer as she listened to him exclaim at every piece his nephew extracted from the box. Was this truly the same man who had ranted at his nephew a short while before?

"Can you show me where you found them?" he asked Philip.

"You want to see?"

Mr Derringer gave a genuine smile that made his eyes crinkle at the edges. "Yes, I want to see. This is a major discovery, and it's all due to you and what an observant young gentleman you are."

The boy swelled with pride at his uncle's words. "Can I show you now?"

"I'm afraid there's not time now, Philip. It's dinnertime. But you can show me tomorrow," his uncle said, "provided Miss Shaw has no objections, and"—he cast Evelina a conspiratorial glance—"you work hard at your lessons all morning."

"Yes, sir," Philip said, beaming from ear to ear.

Mr Derringer ruffled the boy's hair in a friendly manner and together they scooped up the tesserae and replaced them in the box. Evelina observed the connection between them with satisfaction, but also with a touch of wistfulness. The reconciliation had achieved what she had hoped for, but it awoke a yearning, deep inside her. They were a family, and she could not help wishing she were a part of it.

While Philip's head was still bent over the task, his uncle raised his eyes to meet hers again. The warmth in his gaze made her catch her breath, and she responded with a shy smile as an unexpected thought popped into her mind. To marry a gentleman with a ready-made family might not be such a poor arrangement if that man was like Mr Derringer.

CHAPTER 15

The next morning, John awoke with a profound sense of expectation. It was a refreshing change to feel enthusiastic about getting up. He'd never thought there might be Roman remains on Derringer land. It should not surprise him, considering their proximity to Bath. The hot springs had attracted people to the city for centuries.

He had to admit his excitement was heightened by knowing he would not be exploring the Roman remains alone. He wondered what they would find. Together. With Philip. And Miss Shaw.

A brief smile passed across his lips as he remembered the way she'd taken him to task the day before, and the genuine sympathy she'd offered, acknowledging how difficult it had been for him. When she had seen beyond his anger, to the grief buried below.

Her intervention had prevented his stupidity from pushing his nephew even further away from him than he already was. They might have become permanently estranged if she had not stepped in. Instead, she had opened the way for a fresh start with Philip and he revelled in their newfound connection.

After rising early, John forced himself to examine the estate books before breakfast. He opened the ledger and stared at the most recent page, noting the shakiness of the figures, before closing it again. He came to a decision.

It was his policy to take his fences head on, but since taking over Duriel Hall, his resolution had wavered. He'd been overwhelmed with responsibility and—he finally admitted to himself—he'd hoped it would go away.

After yesterday, he no longer wished for that. If he wanted to make a home here for Philip, he must take proper control of running the estate.

The first thing he needed was a new steward. He'd been putting it off. Though Mr Bromley had been the manager for years, he was making mistakes. He wasn't competent at his job anymore.

John took a sheet of paper from his desk and wrote a letter to his brother. Charles had numerous business connections in Bristol and Bath and must know someone suitable.

After breakfasting alone, John returned to his study. He tried to settle down to continue cataloguing the next tray of his collections, but he could not concentrate. Why had he agreed to meet Philip and Miss Shaw in the afternoon? It made the morning seem interminable.

He cleared away the tray and pulled forward the box Philip had left on his desk. One by one, he took the tesserae out and laid them in front of him, recording their size and colour in meticulous detail in his notebook. Underneath each picture, he wrote the words: "Found by Philip Derringer on the Duriel Hall estate." It was strangely satisfying.

For the first time since his brother died, John believed Philip would be all right. He'd spent so many hours dwelling on how impossible it was for him to step into Robert's shoes, he had failed to see what he could offer his nephew. He couldn't replace Philip's father, but he could be a good uncle.

Up till now, he'd done a poor job of it. In fact, he'd made a real mess of it until Miss Shaw came along.

Time dragged by, but eventually the appointed hour arrived, and he climbed the stairs to the schoolroom, with what he hoped wasn't unbecoming enthusiasm. He rapped twice on the door before opening it.

Miss Shaw glanced up with a smile before turning to Philip.

"You may put your work away now. It is time for our archaeological exploration—Roman excavation—call it what you will."

Philip rushed to replace his books on the shelf and then joined John by the door. He studied his uncle's feet and wrinkled up his nose. "Haven't you got any boots?"

John glanced at his shoes. Was there something wrong with them? "Do I need boots?"

Miss Shaw gave a lopsided grimace. "Philip has a point. You may get somewhat damp, so more robust footwear would be preferable."

She lifted her skirts slightly to reveal a pair of sturdy half-boots. "See—I am prepared."

John gulped hard. He saw. An uncomfortable heat rose up his neck as he glimpsed Miss Shaw's legs above the top of her boots.

"I'll change into something more suitable and meet you in the hall," he said, hurrying away before she noticed his embarrassment.

Miss Shaw. He didn't know what to do about Miss Shaw. She got under his skin in a way no other female had ever come close to. But she wasn't interested in trying to attract his attentions. She'd made that abundantly clear from the moment she arrived. However good she was with his nephew—however much she grew to care for the boy—she would not marry John to provide Philip with a mother.

He needed to forget about Miss Shaw and concentrate on being a good uncle. For he doubted she could be persuaded to marry him for any other reason.

Five minutes later, John bounded down the stairs like a schoolboy, dressed for the part in a pair of hessians and a jacket that had seen better days.

"Do you approve?" he asked his nephew.

"Much better, sir."

Philip led the way to the river, leaving John to walk behind with Miss Shaw.

"Your nephew has done nothing but talk of this outing all morning," she said in an under voice. "I hope you realise how important this is to him."

John watched Philip half-walking, half-running ahead in his excitement. He observed the bounce in his nephew's step and smiled to himself. Miss Shaw was doing wonders with the boy. He should not have doubted her. He had not seen him look this animated since—since before his parents died.

They crossed the bridge, and Philip veered to the left and climbed down the bank. John followed close behind. The bank was not steep, but it was rather muddy and slippery because of the rain a few days before. When he reached level ground, he turned and held out his hand to Miss Shaw.

She threw him a quizzical look, as if surprised by his proffered help, but he did not retract his hand, and after staring at it for a few moments, she placed her gloved hand in his and let him help her. John liked the feel of it and was sorry when she stepped onto the ground beside him and withdrew it from his grasp.

Philip waited for them with evident impatience. "Here," he said, pointing to the river bed in front of them. "This is where I discovered the tesserae."

He crouched down and ran his fingers through the water, turning over stones as he went. After a few moments, he squealed with delight and pulled something out of the stream, holding it triumphantly in the air.

"I've found another one," he said, handing the piece to his uncle.

John examined the light brown cube of mosaic in his hands. "You've got a good eye for this, Philip. That's an invaluable tool when you're exploring—far more important than anything else."

His nephew seemed to grow taller before John's eyes at the simple words of praise. Philip straightened up, putting his shoulders back and holding his head high. "Thank you, sir."

John passed the new find to Miss Shaw. "Here. Take a look at this while I inspect the riverbed for myself."

He crouched down next to his nephew and together they rifled through the water. After a while, Philip found another fragment.

"What I can't understand is why these pieces are here —loose," John said.

"Miss Shaw says it is probably because the river

altered its course at some stage, so it ate away at the side of the mosaic."

John scratched his chin. "I wonder..."

He examined the river bank just above the water level.

"See here," he said, pointing to where the earth changed colour. "When the river is swollen after heavy rain, it rises to this point, so it erodes the bank higher up. If this is where the tesserae are appearing, maybe..."

He dug away with his fingers until he found what he was looking for. A piece of mosaic was jutting out from the river bank, but had not become loose enough to fall into the water. "Aha!"

John took a small trowel out of his coat pocket and dug away at the bank until the tessera came loose. He handed it to his nephew.

Philip's eyes shone with excitement. "You found another one."

"I think there are more where this came from."

John climbed back up the bank, again offering Miss Shaw a hand which, this time, she took without hesitation. He started examining the surrounding area.

"Miss Shaw thinks this wall might be Roman," said Philip, clambering up behind him and sitting down on a low wall.

"Miss Shaw seems to be very knowledgeable."

"Oh, she is," said Philip, chattering away. "She doesn't just know about the Romans. She knows all about books and rivers and she even knows the names of the stars. Not all of them, of course. No one could know all of them, except God."

John examined the wall where Philip was sitting. "I think Miss Shaw might be correct, and if she is, then it might belong to the same building as our mosaic. We need spades."

He fetched some tools from the gardener's room and hurried back to where he'd left the others.

They started digging next to the wall in the direction of the river. "Let's see if we can reach the bottom of the wall. Perhaps we'll find some more mosaic," he said.

It surprised John when Miss Shaw peeled off her gloves, picked up a spade, and started digging next to him. When they had dug a channel next to the wall, John took out his trowel and scraped away the dirt from between the stones that had been buried in the earth.

His nephew watched him closely. When John had cleared a course of stones, he handed him the trowel. "You try."

John watched as his nephew copied the technique he'd observed.

"That's right," John said. "Well done. We'll keep digging—you scrape."

After an hour's work, they had uncovered an area next to the wall, but they hadn't reached the bottom. "We're going to have to clear the ground further back," he said, "otherwise the earth will tip into our hole before we find anything."

"I agree," said Miss Shaw. "We don't want to have to re-dig our hole and we'll need to expand it all the way to the stream if we are going to prove a connection between the wall and the mosaic."

John nodded, impressed. "Have you been on an archaeological excavation before?"

Miss Shaw laughed. "No. This is my first."

"Then you have good instincts. Making connections between different elements we discover is crucial. If we find the Roman mosaic on the floor encased by this wall, it proves the wall is Roman, too. The question is, does the mosaic extend this far or not? There is only one way to find out. Let's dig."

Miss Shaw shook her head and laid down her spade. "Not today. It's time we stopped."

"I can dig now if you're tired," said Philip, picking up the spade she'd laid down.

"No, Philip. It's time to stop," said Miss Shaw.

"Do we have to? Please, can we stay a bit longer?" Philip pleaded. John was as eager as his nephew to continue, but he refused to contradict Miss Shaw.

"It has waited hundreds of years undiscovered and can wait until tomorrow," she said.

Philip complained. "But I'm not tired. I can dig some more. It's not getting dark yet. Why do we have to stop now?"

A glance at Miss Shaw's face told John her mind was made up.

He gave his nephew a stern look. "Philip." It was all that was needed.

"Yes, sir," the boy said, his shoulders sagging.

"Cheer up," said John as they returned to the house. "We can dig again tomorrow, provided Miss Shaw says you have completed your studies for the day satisfactorily."

"Really?"

"I promise."

Instantly, the bounce was back in Philip's step, and he skipped along the path ahead of them.

"Thank you," she said, with a wide smile as they parted ways, she to follow her charge, and he to replace the tools in the gardener's room.

John's eyes glowed with pleasure as he stood gazing after them. Why had spending time with his nephew been so difficult before Miss Shaw arrived? Her coming had changed everything.

She had encouraged him to make a home here for Philip. Couldn't he make a home here for her, too? But he mustn't think about that.

CHAPTER 16

*E*velina could not believe the difference in Mr Derringer. Their conversation over dinner was the most animated they had shared. Not even the gloomy presence of Partridge the butler, hovering in the background with a permanent expression of disapproval, was enough to stifle their enthusiasm as they recounted the day's experiences.

"If we find any of the mosaic in situ, I'll invite an expert to examine it," Mr Derringer said as the dessert course was served.

"Don't you consider yourself an expert?" Evelina asked in surprise.

Mr Derringer looked gratified by the suggestion, but dismissed it. "I dabble, Miss Shaw. I prefer a practical approach, touching the actual archaeology. The genuine experts rarely get their hands dirty. They are more likely to spend their days poring over manuscripts and papers written by those who have visited Rome and seen the excavations there. Perhaps if this war is truly over—if we have lasting peace—I could travel abroad..."

As his words hung in the air, his eyes glazed over and the smile—which had sprung to his lips as he shared his enthusiasm for Roman history—faded.

"I suppose that won't be possible now," he said.

"Why not?"

"I thought that was obvious—because I am responsible for Philip."

"You could take him with you. He would love that."

Mr Derringer sat in silence, pondering her words.

"There are too many dangers," he blurted out. "It is not to be considered. I would never forgive myself if something happened to Philip."

Evelina saw the weight of his argument. Not for the first time, she wondered what it had been like for him to gain responsibility for a child overnight. Bringing up his brother's son was a solemn duty to fulfil.

"Maybe when Philip is older," she said, trying to bring the smile back to Mr Derringer's face as she rose to leave him to his glass of port.

"Maybe." But Mr Derringer didn't sound as if he believed it.

❦

ONE MORNING near the end of August, Evelina woke to the sound of rain. Not the light drizzle they had experienced on and off over the previous three weeks, but heavy, unremitting rain. Her spirits plummeted. No digging today—Philip would be disappointed. So was she. Although not averse to giving her aching limbs a break, she would miss being outdoors. If she were honest with herself, she would miss Mr Derringer's company, too.

They had fallen into such a comfortable pattern. Each morning, she taught Philip his lessons, and every afternoon, they worked on the excavation. With the lure of digging up Roman treasures ahead of him, the boy studied hard, eager to be finished before his uncle arrived. Evelina often caught him watching the door for a full hour before the appointed time.

On Sundays, they passed the entire day together. Not digging, but attending morning service at the parish church, sharing a light nuncheon, and then sitting together in the library until dinnertime. They took it in turns to read aloud from books on the library shelves, and Mr Derringer asked Philip about what she had been teaching him.

The boy was a bright student, and he answered his uncle's questions in a manner which did them both credit. Not only did his answers prove he had learned his lessons, but also—for the most part—that he had understood them, too.

After three weeks of digging, they had made excellent progress, uncovering the area of mosaic by the wall before expanding their hole toward the stream. The more they dug, the more the pattern emerged. White and red tesserae formed a chequered border around the edge, with an inner border of smaller, light brown pieces. Within that were even smaller cubes forming white and red swirls interspersed with more light brown tesserae.

It was demanding work and Evelina had never ached so much in her life, but it was worth it. They were working together as a team, and Philip thrived on having so much of his uncle's attention.

As predicted, the boy was so downcast by the rain that Evelina struggled to make him concentrate on his lessons.

She did not expect Mr Derringer to come up to the schoolroom, but at two o'clock, as was his habit, the double knock sounded, and he walked into the room.

"Good afternoon, Mr Derringer," she said. "I did not look for you today as the weather is so bad."

Heat flooded her cheeks as she realised what she'd said. The truth was, she waited for his knock every day as much as Philip, and the only reason she had not looked for it today was because she had convinced herself he wouldn't come.

"We can't go digging this afternoon," Philip said, his face a picture of despair. "Miss Shaw is certain we'll reach the floor level by the stream if we dig for another hour or two. It's not fair."

Mr Derringer raised his eyebrows. "One day of rain will not ruin your life."

"But I wanted to dig today. I can't wait until tomorrow," Philip whined.

"You have to wait. You don't have any choice," Evelina said.

"Why not?" said Philip, going red in the cheeks. He was working himself into a frenzy. "Why can't I dig today? I don't mind getting wet."

"You would not just get wet, Philip—you'd end up covered in mud," his uncle said.

"I like mud. Mother wouldn't have cared if I came back muddy."

Evelina watched as the colour drained out of Mr Derringer's face. He turned away abruptly, as if the words had stirred up emotion he didn't want Philip to see.

She responded to the boy in what she hoped was a helpful way.

"But your mother is no longer with us, and you must respect those who care for you now. It would not be fair on Mrs Partridge if we came back covered in mud."

"I don't care what Mrs Partridge wants," Philip said, his voice getting louder with every sentence. "She hates me. I wish Mother were still alive. It's not fair."

His uncle continued to stare into space. Evelina realised she would have to answer, as her employer seemed lost in his reflections.

But before she could pluck up the courage to speak, Mr Derringer turned back to Philip, a weak smile on his face, as if it were an effort to put it there.

"No, Philip. Life is not fair. If it were fair, your parents would still be alive, and you would not have to live here with me. It's hard to understand why God allows some things to happen, but we can either accept there are things we don't understand and trust God anyway, or we can stay angry. There are some things we cannot change. We cannot bring your parents back, and we cannot alter the weather. But we can thank God for the rain that makes the plants grow and make the most of the day. How would you like to try your hand at fencing?"

Philip took several deep breaths and grew calmer, but he furrowed his brow, as if far from happy.

"Well?" Mr Derringer said, when his nephew remained silent.

"That's kind of you, but I don't want to keep you from your work."

The man blinked, as if surprised by his nephew's response. "I can spare the time."

Philip contorted his features and blurted out, "The truth is...I don't like fencing, sir."

He peered up at his uncle as if he expected a rebuke. Instead, Mr Derringer burst out laughing.

Evelina's chest grew tight as disappointment threatened to overwhelm her. Mr Derringer had been getting on so well with Philip while they uncovered the mosaic that she had not anticipated such heartless behaviour. She had thought better of him. How dare he make fun of his nephew because he disliked fencing?

"Don't look so forlorn, Philip. I'm certain your uncle did not intend to distress you," she said, glaring at her employer, daring him to contradict her.

Mr Derringer shook his head, struggling to suppress his chuckles. "Forgive me, Philip. It seems I don't know you very well yet. I thought I was offering you a treat. It's laughable because I don't care for fencing, either."

Philip's distress melted away in an instant and he grinned at his uncle.

"Would you like to examine some of my collections instead?" Mr Derringer asked.

"Yes, please, sir. Have you got any pieces similar to my tesserae?"

"Let's find out."

The three of them repaired to Mr Derringer's study, where they spent the rest of the afternoon pulling out boxes from his cabinets and examining the contents.

Evelina said little, but it warmed her heart to watch the boy continue to unfurl under his uncle's attention.

"If the rain stops, can we dig tomorrow?" Philip asked.

"Not tomorrow. We're going to Bath."

They were going to Bath? Evelina had to admit a trip to the city would be a pleasant change.

"Do we have to go to Bath tomorrow?"

"Yes. You wouldn't want to disappoint your grandparents. It's weeks since we've visited and now they're back from Weymouth, they want to see you. You'd like to spend time with them, wouldn't you?"

"Yes, but—I wish it was not Wednesday tomorrow."

"Wishing will not change the fact that it is. Besides, don't you think Miss Shaw has earned a day off?"

A wave of loneliness passed over Evelina as she realised the import of Mr Derringer's words. *They* were going to Bath. She was only the governess. *She* would stay here. Alone.

"Miss Shaw could come with us," Philip said.

Mr Derringer opened his mouth to speak, but no words came out. He glanced across at Evelina, a look of apology in his eyes.

She shook off the cloak of loneliness before it suffocated her. This was the life she had chosen. It was foolish to think anything had changed, just because Mr Derringer had listened to her and reached out to Philip.

She swallowed hard. "Not this time, Philip," she said, stepping into the silence before it became awkward. "It is a family occasion, and I'm convinced your grandparents would like to have you to themselves without a stranger getting in the way."

"Oh, I suppose so." The boy's crestfallen expression soothed the pain in her heart. It comforted her that Philip wanted to treat her as part of the family.

What did his uncle think of him championing his governess? She shifted her gaze toward him and was surprised to find him watching her. He nodded his head, a grateful smile on his lips and, she thought, a look of approval in his eyes.

She held his gaze for rather longer than she ought, but if she were honest with herself—which was becoming an increasingly dangerous thing to do—she found it exhilarating to earn this man's approval.

Beneath the surface lurked the question she dared not ask herself. Was approval enough or did she yearn for something more?

CHAPTER 17

*I*t was with considerable reluctance John interrupted their routine to visit his parents in Bath. He was a tad nervous about how his nephew would react away from Miss Shaw's influence and feared he would see a return of the boy's sulkiness on the visit.

He need not have worried. Philip couldn't stop talking during the entire journey into the city. It was a pleasant change, and John leaned against the back of the seat, enjoying listening to him chattering on, answering his questions as required.

How much his nephew had changed since their last trip into Bath, before his parents had gone to Weymouth, a few days after Miss Shaw had come.

When their carriage drew up in the Circus, the door of his parents' house was opened by their elderly butler.

"Good morning, sir, Master Philip," the loyal retainer said, beaming at the pair as they approached the house.

"Good morning, Jeffers," said John, smiling back at

the butler who had known him since he was breeched. "Is it good to be home again?"

"Yes, sir, though I'm still getting used to calling this place home. I miss Duriel Hall," he confessed, "but I would never leave your parents, and truth to tell, the modest size of this establishment is much better suited to my old legs."

"Are my parents upstairs?" John asked. "I expect they are eager to see us."

"Yes, indeed. They are all waiting for you in the drawing room." He nodded to a footman who stepped forward to show them up.

John was still digesting the word 'all' when he and Philip were announced. His gaze took in the occupants of the room. Not only were his parents waiting to receive them, but his brother Charles and his entire family were assembled for the purpose.

"John—how good it is to see you," said Araminta Derringer, rising from her chair and coming toward her son with outstretched arms.

He lifted her hands to his lips and kissed each of them before bestowing a third kiss on her cheek.

She turned to Philip and held out her arms. After a moment's hesitation, he walked into her embrace and gave his grandmother a hug.

"My, Philip, you keep on growing. You look so like your father did at your age."

"Thank you, Grandmother. I hope I will grow up to be just like him."

John greeted his father and Charles with a few words and a nod, but was not surprised when his sister-in-law demanded more. How his sombre youngest brother had won such a vivacious lady as his bride never ceased to amaze him.

"What, no kiss for your sister?" she said, dimpling up at him with a mischievous grin.

"It is a pleasure to see you again, Anne," John said, reaching over the baby in her arms and bestowing a perfunctory kiss on her cheek.

She shot him a speaking look, and he obligingly gave his attention to her child. "It is a pleasure to see you again too, Frances," he said, kissing the baby's forehead.

"That will do for now," said Anne.

"How did you like Weymouth, Father, or should I ask, how did Weymouth like you?"

William Derringer chortled. "I enjoyed the sea air very much, and the sea bathing has had a beneficial effect on my constitution."

"That's good news," John said. "Should I prepare to move out of the Hall so you can take up residence again?"

The moment the light-hearted question was out of his mouth, he wished he could take it back. A pang of remorse assailed him as he noticed Philip's eyes dart anxiously between him and his father, as if the response was important to him. His careless words had rocked his nephew's security. He must take care not to do it again.

The older Mr Derringer shook his head. "I am better —but not *that* much better." He cast a loving glance toward his wife. "We find it suits us, residing in the city with friends all around. The estate is yours to keep."

The tension vanished from the boy's face, and he looked up at his grandfather, his eyes wide with curiosity. "Do you really prefer living here to being at Duriel Hall?"

"Now I am an old man—yes," he replied. "What about you? Do you miss London?"

"I much prefer the country to the town. There's more space to"—Philip scrunched up his shoulders as if struggling to find the correct word—"breathe."

"Does that mean you enjoy living at the Hall?" his grandmother asked.

Philip glanced up at John, and when their eyes met, he gave his nephew a reassuring smile.

"Yes. I do now."

John let out the breath he hadn't realised he was holding.

"I still miss Mother and Father," the boy said in a rush, as if admitting to liking the Hall somehow dishonoured the memory of his parents. "Every day. But it doesn't make me sad all the time anymore. Miss Shaw has helped find things to make me smile again. The best thing of all is I found some Roman tesserae in the stream and Uncle John says he's proud of me, and we've been uncovering a real Roman mosaic with Miss Shaw."

"That's wonderful," she said before transferring her gaze to John. "Who, pray, is Miss Shaw?"

Anne shot him a disconcerting twinkle. "A treasure I found for him."

"A treasure?" his mother repeated, as if she had uncovered a great mystery.

"Miss Shaw is Philip's governess," he said.

"Ah, that would explain it," she replied, as if she accepted his answer, but her eyes said otherwise. John's heart sank as Anne picked up his mother's interest and would not leave the subject alone. He was in no mood to be teased about Miss Shaw.

"Do you deny she is a treasure?" Anne said, fixing him with her penetrating eyes.

John pursed his lips together. What a corner she had backed him into. If he admitted how highly he valued Miss Shaw, his mother would believe him well on the way to getting married and it could only end in disappointment. But to deny she was a treasure? That was unthinkable. His innate honesty won.

"Miss Shaw is an absolute treasure," he reassured both women in as light a tone as he could muster. "She has worked an amazing transformation in Philip, and we are both most grateful she came to our rescue."

"Grateful? You make it sound like she is doing you a favour." His mother chuckled. "Unless I'm mistaken, aren't you paying her for her services?" Her eyes twinkled at him with sudden intuition. "Or am I missing something?"

Drat. Despite his best efforts, he had used an unfortunate turn of phrase and had failed to throw his mother off the scent.

"Oh, as to that, she wasn't a governess before, except to her nephews," Anne said. "In fact, my friend opposed the idea at first. She feared it would look as if her sister couldn't stand living with her, but it wasn't like that. Miss Shaw was eager for the challenge."

His mother's mouth fell open as Anne spoke. She cast a sharp look in his direction, and he knew she would not let it rest.

Sure enough, when they took the air that afternoon, she insisted on taking his arm, while Philip ran on ahead with the others.

"Explain yourself, John," she said. "What are your intentions toward Miss Shaw?"

"Do I have to have any intentions toward her?" John said with a scowl. "She is Philip's governess."

"She is a young lady of good family who has not fallen on hard times."

John huffed. "She chose to abandon that life to teach Philip."

"After living under your roof for months, she won't be able to re-enter that life without causing comment. She may even have difficulty getting another position as a governess. There are few families willing to risk employing a female with the slightest whiff of scandal attached to her name."

He knew his mother spoke from experience and could not treat her comments lightly.

"I appreciate your concerns, but I believe they are needless. Everything is proper. She has her maid with her. I can assure you she is not alone and defenceless in my house."

He paused for a moment and thought of the fiery young lady, who didn't hesitate to take him to task if she felt he had behaved wrongly. Without him realising it, his lips turned up at the corners.

"Aha!" said his mother. "You admire her."

Heat rose up the back of John's neck. He could not deny it. He did admire her—but what had that got to say to anything?

"It matters not a jot whether or not I admire her," he said. "Miss Shaw made her position clear from the start. She is not looking for a husband. If she cares for someone else's children, she would prefer to be paid for it."

"Hmm."

"What do you mean by that?"

"Either she is incredibly naïve or incredibly designing."

John pulled his arm away from his mother and glared at her. "I don't like your insinuations."

She hooked her arm back through his and gave him a soothing look until he started walking along the Royal Crescent again.

"All I'm saying is that if she *were* on the lookout for a husband, she has most cleverly put you off your guard by telling you she isn't. Be careful, John. I would like nothing more than for you to fall in love and marry, and raise Philip in your own family, but I would hate to see you have your heart broken."

John didn't want his heart to be broken either.

———— • ————

EVELINA SPENT the morning writing letters and reading, trying not to picture what Mr Derringer and Philip were doing in Bath. During the afternoon, she gave up trying, and meandered through the grounds, drifting from one place to the next, willing the day to end. Her spirits rose as dinnertime approached—until she remembered she would be dining alone in her room.

She recalled what happened the last time Mr Derringer took Philip to Bath, and resolved to avoid any unpleasantness by staying away from Mrs Partridge, even if it meant going without wine and dessert again. She would not risk causing trouble for Polly. Nor did she wish to witness a repeat performance of the housekeeper's unfeeling behaviour toward her father if he should be visiting her again. No. Evelina would not face Mrs Partridge in her den today, whatever the provocation.

After dinner—which the cook ensured included both wine and dessert—Evelina sat and stared out her bedroom window, trying to make sense of the emptiness inside her.

Had she made a terrible mistake coming to Duriel Hall?

No. God had used her to help heal the rift between Mr Derringer and his nephew, and she could not regret it. But when she chose to become a governess, she hadn't anticipated how tough it would be to accept her loss of status. When Philip was with her, she could almost pretend she was his mother. Today, she could not forget her position, because although she was not teaching, she had not gone to Bath with them. She had been left behind. Alone. And it hurt.

It was the first time she'd questioned the wisdom of her choice to become a governess since those early days, when her room was the sparsely furnished cubbyhole on the top floor, and she'd eaten all her meals with Philip.

Before her room had been switched for the delightful Chinese bedchamber she now called her own. Before she started dining with Mr Derringer.

Unbidden, she let out a heavy sigh as she thought of her employer. She had missed their conversation over dinner. More than that, she had missed—him. What was happening to her long-held beliefs? Was she still averse to the idea of marrying a man who came with a ready-made family? No. For the prospect of marrying Mr Derringer and becoming a mother to Philip was growing more appealing than she cared to admit.

CHAPTER 18

The following Sunday afternoon, John sat in the library with Philip, listening to Miss Shaw read the final chapters of *Pride and Prejudice*—a novel by a lady with rather a wicked sense of humour. The happy conclusion of the story made him wistful.

His mind drifted back to the conversation with his mother. His lips curled involuntarily into a smile as he remembered how she had pounced on the slightest sign that he admired Miss Shaw. He could not deny it—he did admire her. And that admiration was growing into something more.

Despite his mother's warning, he was fast losing his heart to the lady whose expressive voice floated across the room toward him. He couldn't seem to stop himself, although he knew it could only end in heartache. Part of him wished his mother was right—that Miss Shaw might be trying to trap him into marriage. He would be quite content to be trapped by her.

He dismissed the thought as quickly as it came. There was nothing dishonest about Miss Shaw. She would not have lied about not looking for a husband. He must accept they could never be more than friends. That would have to be enough.

Though John found listening to the novel a pleasant diversion, it failed to keep Philip's attention. The boy spoke as soon as Miss Shaw stopped reading.

"A new book has just been published that I would very much like to read," he said. "It's by Lord Harting, and Miss Shaw says he's deeply knowledgeable about Pompeii, even though he's an earl. Do you think we could buy a copy for our library?"

"An excellent idea, Philip. We can walk to the bookshop next time we are in Bath." John hesitated. Wednesday used to be the highlight of his week, but lately it had become just the opposite. It meant a day without seeing Miss Shaw.

He very much wanted to invite her to go to Bath with them, but would she think he was showing too much interest? And what would his mother say, turning up to dinner with Philip's governess? Could he justify her presence because of his nephew?

"Can Miss Shaw come with us this time?" asked Philip before John had found the courage to invite her himself.

John saw uncertainty in her eyes and felt a glimmer of hope.

"Philip, I—"

"What do you say, Miss Shaw?" he said, interrupting before she could give a reason why she couldn't go with them. "Will you come to Bath and take a walk in Sydney Gardens with us?"

Her cheeks turned a becoming shade of pink. "I would very much appreciate the opportunity to make a few purchases and, much as I love digging, a walk would make a pleasant change."

Philip pulled a face. "I would like a copy of the book, but must we walk around the gardens? It doesn't sound very interesting."

"Ah, but Sydney Gardens has more than just flower beds to look at." John leaned toward his nephew as if sharing a great secret. "In the centre, there is a labyrinth."

The boy's eyes lit up. "A maze! Now *that* would be worth seeing. Why haven't you taken me there before?"

"I...I'm not sure. Perhaps I was afraid of losing you."

"Pshaw! You need not worry about me. I bet I can beat you to the middle. You'll see. I'm not the one who will get lost."

John's eyes rested on Miss Shaw's still-flushed countenance as she looked fondly down at his nephew. Philip was right. John was the one who would get lost. His heart would be lost in a moment if Miss Shaw looked at him like that.

◦────•────◦

THE VISIT to Bath was proving delightful. Evelina found it all too easy to forget she was only the governess when Mr Derringer offered her his arm as they walked through the city streets. She had not thought it possible that going shopping could prove such a treat. As she perused the volumes on offer whilst Mr Derringer obtained a copy of the book Philip wanted, Evelina could imagine she was still living in her sister's house and was passing the time as a lady of leisure.

Ever since Mr Derringer had invited her to go to Bath

with him and Philip, she had tried, unsuccessfully, to squash the flicker of hope that he liked her. It was unwise to read too much into the invitation, and she reminded herself, a dozen times a day, that she had no one but herself to blame that she was only the governess. It was the path she had chosen. Her employer was just being kind to her. She must not forget she was there to look after Philip, nothing more.

Evelina was nervous about having to face Mr Derringer's parents. What would they think of him bringing his nephew's governess to dinner? Would she and Philip have to eat separately from the rest of the family? If that happened, she would make sure she never accepted such an invitation again. It was too humiliating to contemplate.

But it was easy to dismiss her misgivings when Mr Derringer seemed intent on treating her like a lady. He insisted on waiting outside with Philip each time she went into a shop. When she had completed her purchases, they walked toward Sydney Gardens. Philip scampered on ahead, eager to reach the maze, and they laughed together at his enthusiasm.

"I thought nothing other than Roman remains would capture his interest," Evelina said. "To recall the labyrinth was an excellent move."

"I wonder whether he'll be so eager when he has spent an hour trying to find his way to the middle," Mr Derringer said, stopping at the booth to purchase their tickets.

As they entered the labyrinth, he leaned toward her, surreptitiously showing her a plan of the maze before tucking it into his pocket. "I bought this too—in case we get lost."

Evelina warmed at his thoughtfulness and even more so at the intimacy of his tone, though the thought of being lost in the maze with Mr Derringer was rather appealing.

The map was not needed. They had underestimated Philip, whose quick mind soon discovered the correct path through the maze. When they entered the central area a moment behind him, they found the boy jigging up and down with excitement.

"Can I have a go?" he asked, pointing to two swing-like structures.

"I see you've found the Merlin swings," his uncle said.

Evelina had never seen one before and eyed the contraptions with interest. Each swing comprised a plank suspended a couple of feet above the ground by ropes at either end, which hung from a frame some ten or twelve feet tall.

"Let me show you how it works," said Mr Derringer with an eagerness that almost matched Philip's own.

Evelina watched as they stood on either end of the board and he showed his nephew how to pull on the ropes to make the swing rock back and forth. As they swung higher and higher, the smile on her employer's face grew. She had never witnessed such a carefree expression on his face before. Why—he was almost handsome.

He drew the swing to a standstill and jumped down. "Now it's your turn, Miss Shaw."

"My turn? You don't expect me to play on the swing?"

"Come on," said Philip. "You feel as if you're flying."

Mr Derringer raised his eyebrows at her. "Afraid?"

"Of course not," said Evelina.

"Then allow me to assist," he said, holding out his hand.

She paused for a long moment, unsure if she should accept. Was this proper behaviour for a governess? She glanced around. There was no one else here in the heart of the maze. They were alone.

After dismissing her qualms, she took his hand and allowed him to help her stand on the swing opposite Philip. She tried to ignore the way her heart beat faster as she leaned on his strength and how sorry she was when he withdrew his support.

"Place your hands on the ropes," said Mr Derringer, "and then pull."

Evelina did as she was told, and the swing began to move. As they worked together, she and Philip rose higher and higher. The boy was right. She felt as if she were flying.

As the swing continued to rock back and forth, her stomach lurched, and she began to feel dizzy.

"Stop, stop, Philip," Evelina called out. "I won't be able to stand up for a month."

Mr Derringer stepped forward and drew the swing to a halt.

She held onto the ropes to steady herself while Philip jumped down.

"That was such fun. I'll race you out of the maze."

"Wait for us," his uncle called, but the boy had gone.

Mr Derringer turned back to the swing and reached out his arms toward Evelina. Putting her hands in his, she stepped down. Her first foot landed firmly, but as the second foot touched the ground, her dizziness caught up with her, and she stumbled forward into his arms.

Heat rushed to her cheeks, and she tried to pull away in embarrassment, but to her surprise, Mr Derringer did not release his grip.

She looked up into his eyes and noticed a warmth in them she had not seen before. A slight smile curved his lips as he bent his head toward her. Evelina felt a tightness in her chest, making it difficult to breathe. He was going to kiss her—and if he kissed her, everything between them would change.

Evelina closed her eyes and waited.

CHAPTER 19

The kiss never came. Mr Derringer let go of her. Even though Evelina's eyes were still shut, the sudden current of cold air that swept over her informed her he had stepped away.

She knew she should feel relieved, but strangely, she regretted he had not given into the impulse to kiss her— an impulse that might have taken her life in a new and unexpected direction. A direction she had hardly dared to consider, but which was growing more appealing by the day.

Stifling the pangs of regret that he had changed his mind, she opened her eyes to a most unwelcome sight. They were no longer alone. Three ladies had entered the centre of the maze.

Evelina had been so focused on Mr Derringer and what he might have been about to do that she had not heard their approach.

One lady stepped toward her. "Miss Shaw? Is that you?"

Evelina's heart sank as she recognised Mrs Franklin—

the least favourite of her sister's friends and the most incurable gossip. How unfortunate she should stumble upon them at such a moment, when they were in what could be deemed a compromising position.

"Good day to you, Mrs Franklin," Evelina said, with as much politeness as she could muster.

The lady bent her head closer, casting a furtive glance at Mr Derringer, who had moved away as she approached. "Forgive me—did I make a mistake? You are still Miss Shaw, are you not? Your sister said you were living in Bath now, but she never mentioned you were married…"

Evelina coloured under the woman's scrutiny, and without realising what she was doing, she cast a desperate look in Mr Derringer's direction as Philip came bursting back through the entrance to the maze.

"Aren't you ever coming?" the boy asked, running up to her and grabbing her hand.

His uncle came up behind him and tapped him on the shoulder. "Miss Shaw has company, Philip."

He coloured. "I beg your pardon."

"Mrs Franklin, may I present Mr Derringer and his nephew, Philip?"

Her employer bowed, and Philip immediately copied him. Despite the awkwardness of the situation, Evelina smiled to herself to see the boy's mimicry.

"Derringer?" Mrs Franklin said. "Are you, by any chance, related to Mrs Charles Derringer?"

"Charles Derringer is my brother."

"Then Philip…?"

"Mr Derringer is Philip's guardian," Evelina said, preventing the need for him to answer.

He bowed his head toward them and drew his

nephew away, leaving her to talk to Mrs Franklin. Evelina wished he had stayed. He could not know how little she relished the prospect of such a conversation, and she was wary of the speculative look in the woman's eye.

"Then Philip's parents?"

"They died last year."

"Oh, I see. I'm sorry," Mrs Franklin said, glancing in Philip's direction with some semblance of compassion before turning back to her. "He's a fine lad."

"If you'll excuse me—" Evelina said, hoping to make her escape, but the woman laid a hand on her arm and continued as if she had not spoken.

"Forgive me for asking"—though Evelina could tell from the gleam in her eyes that she was not—"but I'm curious. Do you have an understanding with Mr Derringer?"

"Why do you ask?" Evelina said, uncomfortable with the way the conversation was going.

"Merely that I am surprised to see you alone together."

"Hardly alone. We have Philip with us. I am his governess."

"The governess—oh—is *that* how it is?"

Heat rushed to Evelina's face as Mrs Franklin's words hung in the air. There was a tightness about the woman's mouth which betrayed her excitement at having captured a tasty morsel of gossip which she planned to enjoy to the full.

It would be all over Bath and half-way to Bristol before dinnertime. The story would get back to Cecilia and she would be upset by having such aspersions cast on her sister's character.

Evelina struggled for breath. How could she refute Mrs Franklin's veiled insinuations?

"Yes, Mrs Franklin. That is how it is," said Mr Derringer, entering the conversation uninvited. Evelina had not even been aware he was close enough to overhear.

"I see you have guessed that Miss Shaw has become more than a governess to us," he continued, placing Evelina's hand firmly on his arm in a possessive way. He fixed his eyes on Mrs Franklin in an imposing manner. "I know we can trust you to keep this to yourself for the time being. Such matters cannot be rushed—because of the boy."

Evelina felt the colour drain out of her face. What was he saying? What had she done?

"Oh, you may trust me, Mr Derringer," Mrs Franklin oozed. "The last thing I would want to do would be to cause you or Miss Shaw any distress."

The woman turned to Evelina, her eyes as wide as saucers, but no longer holding a malicious glint. "How exciting. I thought you were quite set against marriage, but clearly it was just the matter of finding the right man. You can trust me to keep it quiet. How pleased your sister must be for you."

With a knowing smile, Mrs Franklin bade farewell and joined the other two ladies who had, mercifully, remained out of earshot during their embarrassing conversation.

Mr Derringer called Philip over, and the boy ran ahead of them into the maze. As they followed him, Evelina could not resist a final glance at Mrs Franklin and her friends, but she wished she had. To judge from the way the women's heads were bent together, they were already gossiping about her.

Once out of their sight, Evelina tried to withdraw her arm from Mr Derringer's hold, but he held it fast.

She struggled to find the words. "Mr Derringer, I don't know what to say. To have forced you into implying we had an understanding when we have none. It was most obliging of you to quash her slurs on my reputation, but I am only the governess. There was no need for you to say anything, and now, I fear, we are in a worse pickle than before. Mrs Franklin is not known for holding her tongue. Despite her promises, she won't be able to keep such a juicy bit of gossip to herself. I don't know what to do to make it right."

Mr Derringer gave her a wry smile. "I suggest you agree to marry me."

Evelina felt her heart stop. Could she? Did he genuinely care for her, to have stepped in like that to rescue her reputation?

He seemed to sense her hesitation.

"It was my error," he said. "We had grown so comfortable together at the Hall that it never occurred to me that others might view our relationship in a different light. Mrs Franklin's timing was unfortunate, to say the least."

Evelina's bubble popped. Mr Derringer thought it was a mistake—his mistake—that he had been forced to offer for her.

She had thought the worst situation was to marry because someone needed a mother for their children, but she was wrong. It was far, far worse for a man to offer for you because he was obliged to, as a gentleman. There must be some way out of it.

"You're right. It is most unfortunate that she came upon us when Philip was temporarily out of sight—but it is a poor reason to get married. I'll take my chances with my reputation."

Mr Derringer's forehead creased into a heavy frown and his expression spoke of his exasperation, as well as something else she could not quite fathom.

"I, however, am not willing to take any chances with your reputation. I'm sorry the prospect is so distasteful to you, but you really have no choice. You have already told me Mrs Franklin is renowned for her loose tongue. You may be able to live with the slur on your character that would undoubtedly arrive. I cannot."

Evelina refused to look at him. She had turned down offers before because she had not liked the basis on which they were made. This, however, was different. A proposal made with such obvious reluctance was more humiliating than all the others.

"Will you marry me, Miss Shaw?" Mr Derringer asked, forcing out his proposal as though each word pained him.

"It seems I have no choice."

CHAPTER 20

*T*hey walked back through the maze and into the gardens in silence. John wanted to roar with frustration. He desired nothing more than to marry Evelina. But not like this. Not when she had made it so clear that the idea was repugnant to her.

He had grown to care deeply for her and could not bear the thought of her ever leaving. But he had not dared ask her to marry him. He had been certain she would refuse.

And she had tried. Even though her reputation was all but ruined.

He was not surprised she didn't want to marry him. Since she had berated him over his treatment of Philip, their relationship had settled into a comfortable friendship. While he often looked at her, wishing she might be something more to him, he had never expected the same of her.

Although Evelina was somewhat plain in the eyes of the world, John had long since ceased to think of her like that. There was a lot of charm in her character—

the way she would suddenly smile across the room at him, or her face would light up with righteous indignation over some wrong. He admired the way she would fight for what she believed in, no matter what it cost her.

Which was why he knew she would not marry him to be mistress of her own household. Her words to him when she had first come always lurked in the back of his mind. That she didn't want to marry a man to be a mother to his children. That was the arrangement her sister had—the arrangement she was so set against. True, Philip was not his son, but the boy was in his care, which was almost the same.

How could he have been so reckless? When she had fallen into his arms, he had been filled with such intense longing he had lost control. For one glorious moment, when she had closed her eyes, her face tilted upward, waiting for his kiss, John had thought Evelina returned his feelings.

But he must have been mistaken. If she had cared for him, he would not have needed to persuade her to accept his proposal of marriage in order to save her reputation.

If only he had an ounce of the charm Robert had possessed, he would have known how to win Evelina. Even his brother Charles's good looks might have helped gain her interest. But John had neither the charm nor the looks. He had never tried to engage a woman's affections before, and he had failed miserably at his first attempt.

No wonder Evelina had tried to get out of marrying a recluse like himself, with no social graces whatsoever, who couldn't even see across the room without his spectacles.

It was as he had always believed. He was not good

enough for her—but with God's help, he would spend the rest of his life trying to be.

A tiny dot of excitement bubbled up inside him. Evelina *had* agreed to marry him. He would save her reputation and give her a comfortable home. She already loved Philip, and maybe, in time...

The silence between them continued as they walked to the Circus. Philip chattered on, oblivious to the tension between his uncle and his governess.

As they mounted the steps of his parents' house, Evelina would have withdrawn her arm, but John kept it tucked within his own.

"I'm sorry this is not to your liking," he said when Philip was out of earshot, "but if we are to quell the gossips, we must announce our engagement without delay."

Evelina gave a tight nod, but said nothing. It was not encouraging, but John determined to make the best of it.

When they were shown into the drawing room, he was relieved to see his parents were alone. His sister-in-law was too astute for his liking, and no doubt Anne would have read some reluctance in Evelina's mien—a reluctance which John hoped she would forget once they were married.

"So, this is the famous Miss Shaw," said John's mother, stepping toward them and taking Evelina's hands. "I hear you have done wonders with Philip."

Evelina blushed under such praise. "It is a tough thing to lose your mother, especially at such a tender age."

"Indeed, it is, and it would seem you have become a second mother to Philip, as well as his governess."

"I..." Evelina cast an anxious glance up at John.

He took a deep breath. It would be beneficial to get the announcement over and done with.

"Miss Shaw has done wonders for us both, and so we have decided not to let her go." He walked over and took Evelina's hand and gave it a quick squeeze. "I am delighted to inform you that Miss Shaw has agreed to become my wife."

"What wonderful news," his mother said, her face alight with excitement, "and not, I might add, entirely unexpected. I am so pleased, and your sister-in-law will be delighted. It is the very thing Anne hoped would happen."

Evelina's smile turned into a frown. John was not surprised. He did not like to think their union was the result of anyone's matchmaking scheme either.

His mother seemed oblivious to having said anything wrong. She retook her seat on the sofa and motioned to Evelina to take the place next to her. "Come and sit beside me, my dear, and tell me about yourself."

Evelina did as she was bid while John turned to his father, who shook his hand. "Are you sure you know what you're doing?" he asked in an undertone.

John did not know what to say. He knew his parents' marriage was a love match on both sides. He wished with all his heart he could say the same. His eyes rested on Evelina, taking in the myriad of expressions that passed over her face as she talked to his mother.

"Ah, I see how it is," his father said after several moments of silence.

John looked back at him. His surprise must have shown on his face. Had he been asked a question?

"I can see the tenderness in your eyes. She's not a

beauty, but she's got countenance. I see what attracted you."

John could have expanded on Evelina's good qualities, but at that moment, Philip claimed his attention. No one had paid the boy any heed since they had made their announcement. When he saw the whiteness of his nephew's face, John realised their engagement had come as a shock.

His father tactfully moved away so Philip could speak to his uncle alone.

"What is it Philip? Are you unhappy Miss Shaw is going to marry me? I thought you liked her."

His nephew was labouring under some deep emotion. It took him a while to get his words out. "Will you...will you send me away to school now, so Miss Shaw won't have to be my governess anymore?"

It had all happened so fast, John had not had time to give the matter any thought. Wouldn't they continue as they were, with some—rather pleasant—changes?

"I'm certain Miss Shaw will continue to teach you until you go to Eton, but that is not for several years yet." John paused as he questioned his own answer. Perhaps he was wrong. He had not had time to discuss the matter with Evelina. They'd not had time to discuss anything.

"But she won't be able to when you have children of your own. Will you still want me to live with you?"

"Of course, we will," John said, desperately trying not to colour up at the prospect of having his own children—with Evelina. Heavens, he had made such a hash of bringing up Philip until Evelina came along that he didn't trust himself with the task.

"I am your legal guardian, Philip, but I hope you see me as more than that. We are family. Miss Shaw and I cannot ever replace your parents, but we love you and you will always have a home with us—in our hearts and in our house."

John watched as the frown that had clouded Philip's face melted away. Reassured about his future, the boy seemed to dismiss his uncle's marriage from his thoughts, and he spent the rest of the afternoon telling his grandfather about the progress of their Roman exploration.

Meanwhile, John sat listening to his mother draw Evelina out. It was peaceful. He could listen to his two favourite women talking for hours. The thought brought a smile to his lips. His two favourite women. He hoped Evelina would someday hold him in affection, too.

It was encouraging to observe she gave no hint of the reluctance to marry him she had expressed just a short while before. He was proud of her, putting aside her own doubts and embarrassment, so no slur would fall upon their union. It was as if she, too, sensed how important it was to convince his parents that their marriage was based on a sure foundation.

After taking tea, they returned to Duriel Hall. Any hope that Evelina had become reconciled to her lot evaporated as the carriage door shut behind them. Her smile faded, and there was a sadness about her eyes that struck John's heart to the core. His spirits plummeted.

He was betrothed to the woman he loved, but at what cost to her?

EVELINA WAS silent all the way home. Pretending to John's parents that theirs would be a marriage based on mutual affection had taxed her nerves to the full. It was easy to talk of her fondness for John and their mutual love of Philip bringing them together. Of their shared love of history and the excitement of working on the Roman project together.

But it cut her to the quick to hear his mother rejoicing that a lady had finally worn down his defences and made inroads into his heart.

Fortunately, it did not fall to her lot to convince Mrs Derringer that her son held her in affection. His mother seemed to assume that nothing less would have persuaded him into marriage at last. How little did she know...

Every now and again, John cast her a worried glance across the carriage, but a weak smile was the most encouraging response she could muster. He was making the best of it, and she knew she must, too, but not today. She felt too tired.

When they arrived at Duriel Hall, John handed her out of the carriage and tucked her arm in his as they walked up the steps to the house. Partridge held the door open for them and bowed to John, but when he turned in her direction, his eyes dropped to their linked arms, and then jerked up to meet her own with a frosty glare.

Evelina was conscious of the awkwardness of her change in station and pulled her arm away. Their situation would be difficult to navigate until John shared their news with the staff.

She still could not believe it. In one afternoon, she had gone from being a lowly governess to the future lady of the house. She suspected that the servants—the Partridges, at least—would not like it.

"Miss Shaw, perhaps after seeing Philip upstairs, you could spare me a moment of your time," John said, a pleading look in his eyes.

Evelina's heart sank. It was not surprising that John wanted to talk. He wanted to get matters sorted between them. But she could not talk about it—not now. She could not face being alone with John tonight. The pain of realising that marrying her was not John's choice was too fresh.

She raised a hand to her head, which was, in truth, beginning to throb. "Please excuse me tonight, Mr Derringer. I have a headache. Could we talk in the morning instead?"

John gave a brief nod, and moved toward her, as if he were going to kiss her cheek, but—perhaps because of Mr Partridge's gloomy presence—he changed his mind, and merely bid her a good night. "I will see you at breakfast, Miss Shaw."

Falling on her knees by her bed before she slept, Evelina prayed God would give her wisdom. Could she really marry a man who did not love her, or should she run back to her sister's house and hide?

CHAPTER 21

*J*ohn awoke the next morning with a single thought in his head—Evelina. In his mind's eye, he could picture her slender form, working with unmaidenly vigour alongside him at their Roman excavation. He smiled as he thought of her hair coming loose from its pins, her cheeks red from the exertion. And her lips—he gulped—just how long would he have to wait to kiss those lips?

He was sorry the betrothal had been forced upon them, but that did not mean their marriage would not be a success. What better foundation for married life was there than a shared faith, friendship and common interests? And they had Philip. Their mutual love for the boy would continue to draw them together.

John was eager to announce his intentions to his household. It was as if the more people he told, the more certain it was that Evelina would marry him.

He went to his study as usual, but instead of getting out his collections, he rang for a footman to summon Mrs Partridge.

John sat—fiddling with his glasses and twiddling his thumbs—waiting for his housekeeper to arrive. What was the matter with him? He talked with the woman every day. Why did the prospect of telling Mrs Partridge he was getting married make him so anxious? There was an undeniable knot in his stomach. The sooner he shared his news, the sooner it would go.

A knock announced his housekeeper's arrival, and he bade her enter. The woman looked the same as she always did—neatly dressed in black without a hair out of place. Her lips were turned up slightly at the ends, but not enough to tempt John to call it a smile.

Now she was here, he struggled to know how to start. "I have a matter of some delicacy I wish to discuss with you."

Oh dear. That was not the right thing to have said. Mrs Partridge's almost-pleasant expression was replaced by a decided frown.

"There are going to be some changes here at Duriel Hall that might come as something of a surprise to you."

"I hope you are not dissatisfied with my service," she said, challenging John with her eyes.

"You mistake me. The change is not a bad one—and it is about me, not you."

The almost-smile reappeared on her lips, but John felt her hawk-like eyes on him, waiting to hear what he would say next.

"Miss Shaw and I are to be married."

There was a noticeable pause before she responded. Her eyes were wide with what John could only assume was shock. "May I be the first of your household to wish you joy?"

John noticed the woman's lips were pressed tightly

together and sensed, rather than heard, her disapproval. He did not care for it. He realised the news was unexpected, but he had hoped for a more favourable response.

"Is there something else you wish to say?"

"It's just that—" She broke off, lowering her eyes. Was the woman afraid of upsetting him? John thought it better to hear her out rather than guess at what was being said below stairs.

"Yes?"

"Forgive me for speaking freely, sir, but I'm afraid people will talk."

"Why should they talk? It is not an unequal marriage, Mrs Partridge. I am a gentleman and Miss Shaw is a lady."

"But she is the governess."

"And?"

"She's been living under your roof for months. People might say, under your protection…"

A bitter taste filled John's mouth. He knew what the woman was insinuating—that people would think Evelina was his mistress. Was she right? The very idea of people saying such a thing made his blood boil.

"That's ridiculous!"

"Yes, sir," Mrs Partridge said in a soothing voice. "Of course, Miss Shaw didn't mean to trap you into marriage."

John huffed to himself. No. She had not. If that had been her intention, she would have accepted his proposal more readily.

"You can be certain of that. Miss Shaw made it clear to me at the outset she was not on the lookout for a husband," he said.

Something flickered in the back of Mrs Partridge's eyes, making the fluttering in John's stomach increase.

"Say no more. Your actions make sense now." Her smile became more pronounced, though it still didn't reach her eyes.

John wished he understood what she was talking about. "They do?"

"Yes, sir," she said, her voice all innocence. "Treating her as a lady rather than a governess. Now, she is fit to be neither—unless she marries you. And she is so good with the boy, I quite understand why you want to keep her."

The woman fell silent, but her words continued to ring in John's ears. Could his actions really be construed that way? He had ignored his mother's warning that he had compromised Evelina's reputation from the start, thinking her old-fashioned, but perhaps she had been right. What had he done? Was it his actions and not Mrs Franklin's that had forced Evelina to accept his offer of marriage?

He refused to let Mrs Partridge see how much her words had upset him. "Miss Shaw is a treasure," he said, forcing a smile back on his lips, "and I am most blessed she has agreed to make a permanent home here with me and Philip. Please inform the staff of my upcoming nuptials."

"Yes, sir."

"And Mrs Partridge?"

"Yes?"

"What time does Miss Shaw have breakfast? I've asked her to join me in the parlour today."

"At nine o'clock, sir. The same time as Master Philip."

"Then I will breakfast at nine o'clock this morning too."

"Very good, sir."

The door shut behind Mrs Partridge, leaving John alone with his thoughts.

He could not decide which was worse. People thinking that Evelina had trapped him, or that he had trapped her.

CHAPTER 22

*W*hen Evelina awoke that morning, the melancholy of the previous evening had faded, and her normal optimism had reasserted itself. John might not wish to marry her, but he had acted honourably. He had stood by her rather than risk Mrs Franklin destroying her reputation with her careless words.

She still wondered whether it had been necessary. It wasn't as if John had even kissed her.

But necessary or not, the proposal had been made, and their future union assured, even though John had appeared to act out of duty not desire.

She resolved to make certain he never had cause to regret his noble action. She had a lifetime to convince him she was the right woman for him. And she would start today, by talking to him as he had requested.

With fresh resolve, Evelina rang for her maid.

"What time does Mr Derringer take his breakfast?" she asked as Maggie entered the room.

Her maid's eyes were round with curiosity. "I'm uncertain. Do you want me to find out?"

"Yes, please. Mr Derringer has asked me to join him at the breakfast table."

Maggie gave her a knowing look, clearly sensing something was afoot. Though tempted not to rise to the bait, Evelina thought it only fair to tell her maid of her betrothal before word of it reached the servants' hall—if it hadn't already.

"Mr Derringer and I are to be married," she said, hoping that by saying the words aloud, she would start to believe them herself.

A cheeky smile appeared on Maggie's lips. "I knew he was sweet on you."

Disappointment pulled once more on Evelina's heartstrings. How she wished it were true. She ought to dispel the illusion, but she couldn't face it. Maggie was so delighted at the news that she skipped out of the room with such a light step it could have been her getting married, not Evelina.

The maid reappeared a short while later. "Mrs Partridge says the master takes breakfast at ten o'clock."

"Ten o'clock? The same hour as in my sister's household. Plenty of time for me to teach Philip a lesson before I go down."

Without Evelina saying a word, Maggie helped her into one of her prettier dresses and hummed to herself as she fixed her mistress's hair in a more sophisticated style, framing her face with a few loose strands of hair on either side. It was not quite appropriate for a governess, but Evelina would not miss the opportunity to look more attractive to her future husband.

She went up to the schoolroom, hoping for a

semblance of normality in the strange situation in which she found herself. Polly was laying out the breakfast things on the table, and Philip was patiently waiting for her to join him before he started eating.

Evelina smiled to herself. What a long way they'd come since she first arrived.

"You may begin, Philip. I'm taking breakfast with your uncle today."

"Will you take breakfast with him every day from now on?"

"I don't know."

In silence, Philip slowly spread butter on his toast. And then the barrage of questions began.

"Will I get to call you aunt?"

"I hope so."

"Will you still be my governess?"

"Until you go to Eton."

"Will you and Uncle John have lots of children?"

Evelina turned away as the colour rushed into her cheeks unbidden. She had not even got used to the idea she was going to marry John. As for more intimate matters...

"I don't know."

"I'd like to have lots of children," Philip said, seemingly oblivious to her discomfort as he munched his way through his toast. "It would be more fun with brothers and sisters to play with. Do you have any brothers or sisters?"

Evelina's heat faded as she told Philip about Cecilia and her family. His interest in her sister's stepsons provoked enough questions to keep them going until breakfast was over without reverting to more personal questions, which she did not know how to answer.

Once Polly had cleared the breakfast things, Evelina attempted to teach a lesson, but she found it hard to concentrate. Several times her attention drifted, and she had to get Philip to repeat what he had said. She was relieved when Maggie came to the schoolroom, as requested, shortly before ten o'clock.

"Now, I want you to complete all the sums on this sheet while I am talking to your uncle. Mind you don't tease Maggie. Be as good for her as you are for me."

"Yes, Miss Shaw."

After leaving Maggie to watch over Philip, Evelina descended the stairs. As she neared the breakfast parlour, her stomach tightened. Had John really asked her to marry him or was it all a dream?

It was fortunate she had agreed to meet him at the breakfast table. She wouldn't be able to concentrate on anything until they had talked. It would be agony to wait until the afternoon to see him again. And it would be better if they met, for once, without Philip's eyes upon them.

As Evelina entered the room, her heart sank. Mr Partridge was directing a servant to clear the dirty plates from the table. Had John eaten without her?

After standing in awkward silence for several moments, she plucked up the courage to address the butler. "Has...has Mr Derringer come down to breakfast yet?"

"The master took his breakfast at nine o'clock," the man said in his normal dreary voice.

"But Mrs Partridge told my maid he ate at ten."

"He normally does. But today, Mr Derringer took breakfast at nine."

Evelina bit back her irritation. Had the housekeeper deliberately given Maggie the wrong time?

Determined not to retreat in disgrace, Evelina sat down at the table and forced herself to eat a piece of toast and a lukewarm cup of tea that she poured herself from the pot. After her brief repast, she left the room, but instead of returning to the schoolroom, she headed for Mr Derringer's study. Their conversation was important. Philip's lessons could wait.

As she exited the breakfast room, Evelina almost bumped into Mrs Partridge. Dare she confront the woman about giving her maid the wrong time?

Before Evelina could decide, the housekeeper addressed her. "Am I to wish you joy, Miss Shaw?" she said in a dour voice. "The master says you're to be married."

It appeared that John had already told the servants.

"Yes, we are," Evelina said, a shy smile on her lips.

The housekeeper tilted her head to one side and gave Evelina a pained look. "That's right, miss. Put on a brave smile and make the best of it. How wise of you not to take it to heart that the master is only marrying you out of duty."

Evelina's smile vanished. What had John told this horrid woman? One of the first things she would do as mistress of Duriel Hall would be to replace this hateful housekeeper and her miserable husband.

"I am certain Mr Derringer would not be pleased to hear you talk like that."

"Forgive me. I meant no disrespect. You did not think he was marrying you for some other reason, did you?"

Heat flooded Evelina's cheeks. Yes, John was

marrying her out of duty, but somehow Mrs Partridge's words turned his honourable proposal into something sordid.

"Oh, come, Miss Shaw. You can be honest with me. You must have known from the start Mr Derringer would be honour-bound to marry you—a single lady of good family living under his roof."

"I knew no such thing. I came to look after Philip—as his governess."

"Of course you did, and the boy dotes on you. I don't blame you for wanting to become his mother..."

"That was never my intention, Mrs Partridge. I told Mr Derringer from the start I was not interested in such a marriage."

"Forgive me. I assumed—but if that is the case, you have my sympathy..."

Why was the woman offering her sympathy? What was she implying?

Mrs Partridge shook her head from side to side, a pitying expression on her face. "You poor girl."

"I don't understand. What do you mean?"

"That if you had no desire for marriage, it would have been better for you if you'd never crossed the threshold of Duriel Hall. You've succeeded so well with the boy that the master would never let you go, whatever it takes..."

Evelina walked away before her temper got the better of her. How dare Mrs Partridge say such things about her and John? Is that really how it seemed to the hateful woman? Evelina's stomach turned sour at an even worse thought. Had Mrs Partridge poured her poisonous words into John's ears too?

She hurried along the corridor toward John's study.

She needed to speak to him, to explain why she had not joined him at breakfast, and, if she could, to find out whether he believed she had tricked him into marriage. Because if he did, she would break off the engagement.

Her pace slowed as she thought of the alternative. What if John had set the trap? Was that why he had been about to kiss her? To make it impossible for her to refuse his proposal? No. She would not believe that of him. He would not stoop so low—would he?

She raised her hand, ready to knock on the door of his study, when she heard voices within. Bother. She would have to wait. John was not alone.

CHAPTER 23

*J*ohn was ensconced in his study with his new estate manager, and he was not enjoying it one bit. He thought that if his spirits sank any further, they would hit the floor. How had a day which had started with such hope gone downhill so fast?

First, his housekeeper had made him wonder whether it was his own careless behaviour that had made it impossible for Evelina to refuse his hand in marriage, quite apart from any damage that Mrs Franklin might have done.

Then, instead of having a chance to dispel his fears by talking to his betrothed, Evelina had failed to join him at breakfast. He had sat at the table until half-past nine, waiting, before he reluctantly faced the fact that she wasn't coming. If he had been braver, he would have sent a servant to her room to remind her of his request for her to join him.

But he was a coward in his own house and had forced himself to eat a slice of toast and gulp down a cup of coffee before hiding away in his study.

Finally, Mr Walker had arrived. John had taken on the young man as estate manager the week before, at the recommendation of his brother. It was not a moment too soon. Mr Bromley's health had deteriorated so rapidly that John had already relieved him of his duties and settled him in a comfortable cottage on the estate, where the old man had passed away a few days later.

John had visited him the day before he died. In a moment of lucidity, Mr Bromley had begged his forgiveness for making a mess of things, and when he had given it, the man had sunk into a peaceful sleep from which he never woke.

Since his appointment, Mr Walker had been examining the accounts. Today, he had come to John with his findings, and they were most unwelcome.

"The estate is not in as good a shape as it should be."

John felt a sharp stab of guilt. He had relied on the long-standing estate manager, though he knew he was past his best. If John had taken up his responsibilities wholeheartedly from the start, this would not have happened. Instead, he had put it off, hiding from issues he should have faced.

"It is as I feared then—Mr Bromley was bungling the accounts." He hesitated, not wanting to hear the answer to the question he knew he had to ask. "How bad is it?"

Mr Walker smiled for the first time. "The damage is not irreparable. The estate income is satisfactory, but it cannot sustain the current level of expenditure."

Worry creased John's brow. Such a thought had never occurred to him. "That is troubling."

"Would you allow me to suggest where we might make some economies?"

John sighed. "I have just become engaged to be

married, and had thought to increase the household expenditure, not reduce it."

"Congratulations," said Mr Walker. "I hope you will not think me mercenary if I ask whether the young lady comes with a dowry."

John felt the heat shooting up the back of his neck. "No." Why was it so difficult to admit? "No dowry. I am marrying Miss Shaw—my nephew's governess."

Mr Walker chuckled. "There's an economy I hadn't considered. At least you'll be saving the governess's wages."

John did not laugh. This interview was not the least bit amusing. He glowered at the man, and the estate manager hurried on. "Shall we go through the accounts together and look at those areas of expenditure I think we could reduce?"

John nodded. What else could he do? He must ensure that the Duriel Hall estate could sustain itself for future generations.

"The household expenses have increased significantly compared to what they were before you took over."

"That may be because of the change in housekeepers," John said. "Mrs Partridge took over the role when I came to the Hall. She might not be as thrifty as her predecessor, but she puts such excellent dinners on the table that I have not cared to complain. Mr Bromley was forever moaning about how the war has put prices up."

Mr Walker raised his eyebrows at that, but let it pass. "By far the largest expense is your household staff. I have compared the sum drawn to pay the wages bill each quarter for the last few years and wondered, perhaps, with your—um—lack of experience, you employed more staff than you needed when you took over running the estate. Are there any servants you could do without?"

John let out a despairing huff. "I have not taken on any new servants, bar the housekeeper and butler that Mr Bromley employed to replace those that went with my parents. And, of course, Philip's retinue and my manservant. Are you suggesting I should dismiss my valet or my nephew's nurse?"

Mr Walker screwed up his face in confusion. "That's strange. Why is the wages bill so much higher for the last few quarters then?"

"I don't know," said John. "I'm afraid to say—to my shame—that I never questioned it. I trusted old Mr Bromley. He had been my parents' steward for decades."

"I have a bad feeling about this," said Mr Walker.

John didn't know what the man was talking about. "Are you going to enlighten me?"

"Let's go through the wages first, sir. I don't want to share my misgivings until I've got some proof."

John did not like the sound of that.

Mr Walker read out a list of names and the amount each of them had been paid on the last quarter day. John acknowledged each one with a nod. It seemed like a pointless exercise and the rhythmic sound of the steward's voice was more likely to send him to sleep than throw up any mysteries until he heard Knight's name for the second time.

"Stop. You're repeating yourself."

Mr Walker shook his head, his lips pressed tightly together. "Do you have a second man named Yates and another called Stevens?"

"No. Only one man by each of those names."

"And yet, their names are entered twice. It is as I

feared. You've been paying three servants who don't exist. It looks like someone was embezzling estate funds. Perhaps your previous steward was pocketing the money to feather his nest for his imminent retirement."

"I find that hard to believe. It must be just an error. The man was getting senile—inept, but not dishonest."

"Then where, Mr Derringer, are the surplus funds?"

John had no idea.

CHAPTER 24

*E*velina abandoned any attempt to talk to John and returned to the schoolroom. If she concentrated on teaching Philip, she might be able to ignore the unsettled state of her mind—and the ache in her heart.

She was relieved to find the boy had behaved himself in her absence and completed the work she had set.

"Excellent, Philip. Let's see how much you remember of our last geography lesson." She led him to one side of the room where a magnificent pair of globes stood—one showing the countries of the world and the other the stars in the sky.

"Can you find where we live?"

Philip turned the terrestrial globe around with two hands until he found Europe. "There," he said, putting his finger on England.

"What about Waterloo, where Wellington won his magnificent victory over Napoleon?"

Philip moved his finger across until he found France

and then settled on a spot just below the word Holland. "Here?"

"Very good. What about Rome?"

As she continued with her lesson, Evelina relaxed. There was something soothing about teaching Philip. It was as if nothing unusual had happened yesterday and they could carry on as before. She could ask questions and applaud her pupil's progress. She was proud he had learned to recite the kings and queens of England with very few mistakes.

After a light nuncheon, they turned their thoughts to the Romans, both of them waiting for John's knock.

When two o'clock came and went, Evelina feared her betrothed was avoiding her, offended she hadn't joined him for breakfast. If that were so, it did not augur well for their marriage—if there was to be a marriage.

Philip propped his elbows on the desk and rested his chin on his hands. "Why hasn't Uncle John come?"

"I expect he had business to attend to. Shall we work on our mosaic by ourselves?"

"I suppose," said Philip, pouting, "but it won't be the same."

No, it wouldn't be the same. Nothing was ever going to be the same again. With a brightness she was far from feeling, Evelina encouraged Philip to join her for a walk down to the ruin.

There was a decided chill in the air. Summer was over, and Evelina feared they would not have many more days that year to work on their excavation. Philip's spirits seemed to revive once they were outside, and he skipped down the path in front of her. Spades in hand, they walked to the river and started to dig.

After half an hour's digging and another half hour

looking for tesserae in the river, Evelina's hands were so cold she could barely feel them. The shadows were lengthening, and she knew it would soon get dark. As always, when she suggested they stop, Philip objected.

"Just a bit longer—Uncle!"

Evelina had been so intent on the coldness of her hands that she had not heard John's approach.

"I'm sorry I couldn't join you today," he said to them. He smiled at Evelina, but she thought it looked false, as though it were an immense effort. As though he were resigned to his fate, but not happy about it. The ache in her heart came back with full force.

Philip offered his uncle his spade, but John refused to take it. "Don't be selfish, Philip. It's time to go inside. Can't you see Miss Shaw is cold?"

Evelina noticed Philip's anxious eyes glance at her and back to his uncle. "Yes, of course, sir," he said, climbing out of the ever-widening hole they were digging, which nearly stretched to the stream.

John examined their progress. "One more day should do it."

"We could have finished today if you'd been here," Philip said in a downcast voice.

"Then perhaps we should celebrate before we dig the last section," said John. "Would you like to take your dinner with us in the dining room tonight, Philip?"

The boy's eyes almost burst from their sockets. He gulped hard. "Yes, sir, if you are certain. I don't think my table manners will disgust you."

Evelina's heart warmed to see John reaching out to his nephew. Their relationship was still so new—so fragile—that it would not take much for Philip to feel unwanted again. What better way to show his nephew how important he was to him?

She tried to stoke the warmth in her heart, dwelling on John's relationship with Philip and trying not to think of his relationship with her. But it was impossible. She could not ignore the facts. By inviting Philip to join them at dinner, John was avoiding having to talk with her alone. The ache in her heart deepened.

John picked up the spades in one hand and offered her his other arm. Evelina took it, but felt no connection with the man she was to marry. It felt as though he were drifting away from her.

Philip took her other hand. "You must tell me if I do anything wrong," he said in an urgent whisper.

Evelina assured him she would, and some of the warmth returned. Philip loved her—needed her—even if his uncle didn't.

CHAPTER 25

*A*s she lay in bed the next morning, Evelina wondered whether the day would be as difficult as the last. It had not all been bad. She smiled as she remembered Philip's excitement at joining them at dinner for the first time—so grown up and yet so insecure, so afraid of doing something wrong. John had dedicated himself to putting his nephew at ease, and the boy had soon unfurled, chattering away in his normal manner.

She had contributed little to the conversation, and only by the occasional smile in her direction did John show he thought of her at all.

But though he smiled at her, the drawn look on his face did not lessen, and she felt responsible for those frowns which reappeared when he thought no one was looking.

Evelina knew she should talk to John, but could see no solution to their situation. How could she free him from having to marry her when he was so determined to save her reputation, however much it went against his inclination?

It had been weak of her, she knew, but she had taken the cowardly route, pleading another headache and retiring with Philip—putting off the conversation to another day. At least John had made it clear he would take breakfast at nine o'clock, so there was no chance of missing him.

Once dressed, Evelina headed for the schoolroom, as usual. There would be time for a lesson before she joined John at the table.

"Good morning," she said as she walked through the door—but her pupil was nowhere to be seen. She wondered where he could be. It had been many weeks since he last played truant.

Philip had been disappointed John had not joined them the previous afternoon, but he had seemed so content at dinner that she had not expected any trouble.

Could he still be upset? Surely not. But if he was still upset, she knew where he would be—fighting with the stable boy.

Evelina hurried down the stairs and across the hall to the rose drawing room. As she stepped out onto the terrace, she heard the unmistakable sound of Philip's voice coming from the direction of the stables.

On entering the yard, Evelina saw the sight she had been dreading. Philip and the stable boy were rolling in the dirt together, pounding each other with their fists—and the housekeeper had reached them before her.

"What is the meaning of this?" said Mrs Partridge, grabbing Philip by the scruff of his neck and pulling him to his feet.

The other boy ran off without a backward glance.

"Fighting again," the woman said, shaking her head. "No wonder Miss Shaw despairs of you. She will send you off to school in the blink of an eye once she has married your uncle."

Evelina gritted her teeth. How dare that woman put such thoughts into the boy's mind?

"Thank you, Mrs Partridge. I can take it from here," she said, refusing to react to the look of loathing the housekeeper cast in her direction. It was no more than she had come to expect.

The woman released her grip on Philip, and he ran to Evelina's side and slipped his hand in hers.

Evelina waited for Mrs Partridge to leave before speaking to Philip.

"I thought you understood that fighting was not acceptable," she said, unable to keep the disappointment out of her voice.

Philip's mouth turned down at the ends, but he said nothing.

"Don't you have anything to say?"

"I was upset."

"So, instead of waiting for your lessons to begin, you came down here looking for a fight?"

"No."

Evelina raised her eyebrows. It seemed unlikely, given Philip's penchant for fighting.

"It's true. I don't tell fibs."

"Then what were you doing down here when you were supposed to be in the schoolroom?"

"A maid came with a message saying that Mrs Coombes needed her basket back—the one I borrowed to collect blackberries in. I'd forgotten all about it. I thought I had time to return it and get back to the schoolroom in time."

"Why didn't you just give the basket to the maid?" she asked in exasperation.

"Mrs Partridge said I had to bring it down myself and apologise for not returning it earlier."

Evelina thought that was just like the woman—trying to be difficult. "That still doesn't explain why you were fighting."

"I told you—I was upset."

"Why? Are you still cross with your uncle for being too busy to dig with us yesterday? You can't lash out every time someone lets you down."

"Not that," said Philip. "It was what *she* said."

Evelina did not have to ask who 'she' was. Mrs Partridge. What had she been saying to upset Philip now? The woman would have to go.

Evelina examined Philip's face. There were scratches down one cheek and an ugly red mark under his right eye.

"Come on," she said, leading the way back to the house. "We had better see to that eye. Mrs Coombes might be able to give us some ice to put on it."

They walked around to the far side of the house, and Evelina entered through the kitchen door with a reluctant Philip in tow. Mrs Partridge was standing to one side of the room, talking to her husband.

Evelina ignored them and addressed the cook. "Have you any ice left, Mrs Coombes?"

"Yes, Miss Shaw, though not a huge supply, and there'll be no more till the winter sets in. What do you want ice for, anyway?"

Evelina pulled Philip forward. "I've found a lump of

ice wrapped in a cloth to be an effective way of reducing swelling."

"Oh, my," said the cook, looking at Philip's face. "That'll be a mighty fine bruise. There'll be enough loose ice left for that without needing to send Yates with his pickaxe. If you wait a few minutes, I'll find someone to—oh, Polly," she said, beckoning over the maid who had just walked into the kitchen. "Please, could you get some ice for—"

"I imagine Miss Shaw can get the ice she needs for her pupil without disturbing your work or Polly's," said Mrs Partridge, who had clearly been listening to their conversation.

"I don't think Miss Shaw should—"

"Is there a problem, Mrs Coombes?"

The cook shot Evelina an apologetic look.

"I can manage," said Evelina, keen not to get the cook into trouble with the housekeeper. How hard could it be to fetch some ice? "If you give me a bucket and trowel, I'll go myself."

"Are you certain? I don't think Mr Derringer would be happy—"

"I'll be fine," Evelina said.

The cook went over to a cupboard and brought out a metal bucket and trowel, and handed them to Evelina. "Here you are. Do be careful—and don't catch cold down there."

Evelina turned to leave, but the cook called her back.

"You'll need a lantern too, madam, or you might fall and break your leg." Mrs Coombes lifted an oil lamp down from a shelf and lit it with a taper from the fire before handing it to Evelina.

She thanked her and led Philip back out into the corridor.

"I was disappointed to find you fighting again."

"I'm sorry, but—"

Evelina put up her palm to silence his excuses.

"I know you were upset, but it is better to talk about your feelings rather than taking out your distress on someone else. It is important you realise that. There will be no digging today. Go up to the schoolroom and wait for me, and I'll join you once I've got some ice."

"But that's not fair."

"There's that word again," she said, shaking her head. "No, Philip. It may not seem fair to you, but it wasn't fair to hit the stable boy when it was not him you were angry with."

He wriggled uncomfortably. "I suppose not."

"Off you go. I won't be long. The digging will still be there tomorrow."

Evelina watched as Philip dragged his feet along the corridor toward the stairs. She waited for him to turn the corner before walking back through the kitchen to the back door.

Once outside, she headed for the icehouse. The red brick structure lay at the bottom of a shallow slope, not far from the Hall. As she walked through the arched opening and entered the tunnel-like corridor which led to the storage area, she shivered. The thick walls which did such an excellent job of keeping the ice from melting also kept out the comparative warmth of the autumn weather. It must have been pleasant to step inside on a hot day, but at this time of the year, it was decidedly chilly.

Evelina put down the lantern and bucket whilst she

lifted the bar and pulled the heavy wooden door open. She stood on the threshold, holding up the lantern so she could see inside. As her eyes got used to the gloom, she gasped.

No wonder Mrs Coombes had not wanted her to fetch ice for herself. She was standing at the top of a deep, round brick-lined pit, which fell some twenty feet below her. The only way down was a flight of wooden steps, almost as steep as a ladder. For a moment, she considered retreating, but the thought of Mrs Partridge's sneers if she returned empty-handed spurred her on.

She dared not climb down holding the lantern and so she searched for a place to hang it, where it would provide her with the most light. Just inside the doorway, she found a hook on the wall, and she hung it there, hoping it would enable her to see well enough at the bottom to get some ice. With the bucket hooked over her arm, she descended backwards, one step at a time, into the gloom.

At the foot of the stairway, she waited for her eyes to adjust to the darkness and then looked around. In front of her, the floor was covered with dirty straw mixed with damp sawdust. Against the far wall, she spied a modest pile of fresh ice left over from the previous winter.

With small steps—trying to avoid the worst of the sludge—she made her way over to the last of the useable ice. She should not have been in such a hurry to come down here. The hem of her dress would be sodden by the time she finished. She should have sent a manservant. After all, once she was married to John, they would be her staff, to direct as she willed without bowing to the dictates of Mrs Partridge.

Evelina found some loose pieces of ice and shovelled

a couple of scoops into her pail. As she turned to go, her foot slipped. She dropped the bucket, and only just stopped herself from falling flat on her face. Her hands landed heavily on the soggy carpet of slush, breaking her fall.

Evelina was rapidly going off icehouses. The sooner she got out of this freezing gloom, the better. After picking herself up, she located the pail, which mercifully still had ice in it.

Disoriented, she turned around in a circle. She could see the glow of the lantern, but not the daylight from the open door beside it. It was only then she realised that there was no daylight. Someone had shut the door.

CHAPTER 26

*J*ohn sat in the breakfast parlour, tapping his fingers on the table with growing impatience. His temper was on a short rein, as he had not slept well. He had dwelt on his meeting with Mr Walker for a long time after extinguishing his candle, and concluded that his estate manager must be right. Because of John's negligence and misplaced trust, old Mr Bromley had stolen more than double his income from the estate over the last year. That he had not lived to enjoy his ill-gotten gains did not appease John one bit.

John was to blame, and he would allow himself to feel it.

At least he could assure Evelina the estate was in expert hands now. He drummed his fingers on the table again. Where was she? Evelina had apologised for failing to meet him at breakfast the previous day, claiming she had mistaken the time, but that apology sounded hollow now. Today, there could be no mistake over the hour, and she still wasn't here.

Why wouldn't she talk to him? Was the thought of

marrying him so repulsive to her? Even if she didn't love him, was she not the least bit grateful to him for saving her reputation?

John pushed back his chair with sudden force and rose from the table without eating. He would confront Evelina. Now. This conversation had been put off for far too long.

He climbed up the stairs and walked along the corridor to her room. He hesitated for a moment and then rapped twice on the door. That was how he always knocked when he went up to the schoolroom.

It was opened almost immediately, but not by Evelina, by her maid.

Maggie bobbed a curtsey, her eyes wide open in surprise. "Can I help you, sir?"

"Um...I would like to speak to Miss Shaw. Is she in her room?"

"No, sir." She screwed up her face in concern. "Didn't she come to breakfast? She told me she had time to give Master Philip a lesson as usual before coming down to join you."

"She did not. I suppose she must have forgotten the time—again."

Maggie coloured and looked as if she would defend her mistress, but John was in no mood to listen to excuses. He turned on his heel and mounted the second flight of stairs to the schoolroom. This time he did not knock, but threw open the door and burst into the room. It was empty.

He frowned. Where was Evelina? Where, for that matter, was his nephew? His chest tightened as an unpleasant thought came to him. They were only a day's digging away from uncovering the entire mosaic. They wouldn't have gone to finish it without him, would they? Did they think he wasn't interested because he had let them down yesterday?

He hurried back down the two flights of stairs and out of the house and strode down the familiar path to the stream, but when he reached the site of the mosaic, there was no one there.

"Philip? Miss Shaw?"

No answer.

It was a comfort to think they did not want to exclude him from the last session of digging, but it did not tell him where they were.

John marched back to the house and stormed through the front door. He asked the footman on duty whether he had seen Philip or his governess.

"I've not seen Miss Shaw, sir, but I saw Master Philip earlier."

"Where did you see him?"

"He was going downstairs with a basket at about eight o'clock, but I didn't see him come back again. I wasn't in the hall all morning, though, as I was running errands for Mrs Partridge."

John frowned. He would have to remind his housekeeper that his footmen were not her personal servants.

But he was getting distracted. If Stevens had seen Philip heading for the basement, Mrs Partridge might know where he was.

John sped down the staircase to the housekeeper's room and knocked on the door.

"Why, Mr Derringer, whatever brings you below stairs?" the woman asked, stepping out of her room and closing the door behind her.

"Have you seen my nephew?"

"Why, yes, I have. Cook said he borrowed a basket weeks ago, and I asked him to return it without delay. He brought it down here before breakfast." She let out an exaggerated gasp. "Don't say he's run off again, sir. Not when Miss Shaw was doing so well with him."

John bit back his irritation at the veiled slur on Evelina's ability to control Philip's behaviour.

"Did Miss Shaw come down here looking for him?"

"Yes, she did."

John was becoming exasperated. The woman clearly knew something—why didn't she just tell him?

"Did she find him?"

"Yes. We both did. In the stable yard. He was fighting again, and Miss Shaw was none too pleased about it. I'm afraid there was an altercation between them. 'No digging today.' Those were her very words—I couldn't help overhearing—and if you ask me, Master Philip was mighty angry about it, saying it wasn't fair. I do hope—but no. He wouldn't revert to his old ways, would he...?"

John had to admit it sounded like his nephew—or at least, the way he used to behave. But if Evelina had found him, why weren't they in the schoolroom?

"Did they go back upstairs?"

"Miss Shaw told Master Philip to return to the schoolroom and wait for her, but I couldn't say whether or not he did, as I went back into my room. I suppose he would have obeyed his governess, but then again, he was so cross at being told there would be no digging today, there's no telling what he might have done once my door was closed."

John let out a heavy sigh. Could his nephew really have reverted to how he was before Evelina had come?

They had developed such a good relationship with Philip that there had been no need for discipline. Until now. It didn't look promising if the boy had been found fighting again. Had he rebelled the first time he had been punished? Had his good behaviour hidden the fact that he had not changed inside?

It was challenging to admit, but John knew he'd been too soft on his nephew. His bad habits should have been stamped out before they had taken root—long before Evelina had come to Duriel Hall.

Philip had got away with too much for too long. He had been through so much that John had not wanted to add to the boy's woes by punishing him for his outbursts of anger and for running away from his governesses. And John had sympathised with him. He'd often wanted to hit something in the early days of his grief, and had constantly faced the temptation to hide in his work.

But it had been a mistake to ignore Philip's behaviour, and he had not been helping his nephew. Firmer boundaries would have helped make him feel more secure, and he would not have reverted to his old ways at the first sign of opposition.

"What about Miss Shaw?" he asked, his voice sharper than before. "Where did she go?"

"I believe she was heading to the kitchen, sir."

With a nod, John strode down the corridor to the kitchen and stood in the doorway.

"A word with you, Mrs Coombes."

The cook hastily wiped her hands on her apron and hurried over, an anxious expression on her face.

"Have you seen Miss Shaw?"

The woman's face relaxed when she realised John was not cross with her.

"Not in the last hour, sir. Not since she came in to get some ice."

"Some ice? Why did Miss Shaw need ice?"

"Master Philip had a bruise on his cheekbone and Miss Shaw seemed to think putting ice on it would help."

"I see—and did you give her some?"

Mrs Coombes blushed. "I was a mite busy, and Mrs Partridge didn't want me or Polly to leave the baking, so Miss Shaw said she would go herself."

John raised his hands in the air and dropped them again. "She what? Wasn't there anyone else who could have gone? Oh, never mind. Thank you, Mrs Coombes. You've been most helpful."

He exited through the back door and strode down the path toward the icehouse. When he reached it, John peered through the archway and saw that the door was shut. Thinking Evelina must have long since returned to the house, he was about to turn away when he thought he heard a noise.

Alarm coursed through his body. The sound came from inside the icehouse. He hurried forward, lifted the wooden bar, and opened the door.

"John, thank heavens," said a pale-faced Evelina, stumbling forward into his arms.

Such an intense wave of relief passed over John that he almost cried out. The relief was mingled with something warmer as he glowed to hear her use his given name for the first time. He put his arms around her and rubbed her back as she let out a few convulsive sobs.

"You're safe now. I've got you."

After a while, Evelina's body stopped shaking, but John was in no hurry to let her go. He ran his hand down the side of her cold cheek, and she gazed up at him, a curious look in her eyes he could not quite fathom.

John knew that if she continued to look at him like that for much longer, he was going to kiss her. At this moment, he could almost believe she cared.

His eyes dropped to her lips, still slightly purple from the cold, and he imagined what it would feel like if they met his. He decided he could not wait any longer to find out.

He took off his glasses and gazed into her deep brown eyes. As he lowered his head toward her, she closed them, and their lips met—the warmth of his touching the chill of hers. She tasted sweeter than an ice from Gunter's.

He pulled away for a moment to look at her, hardly daring to believe she was here, kissing him of her own free will. Her eyes flickered open and what he saw in their depths gave him hope that perhaps—despite everything —there might be love in their future together.

John reached up his hand and cupped her cheek and was about to lean in and capture a second kiss when he glimpsed a figure out of the corner of his eye. Mrs Partridge stood at the top of the slope leading down to the icehouse.

He stepped away from Evelina and quickly replaced his spectacles, embarrassed to have been discovered in such a position, even with the woman he was going to marry. A becoming red glow suffused Evelina's cheeks, suggesting she felt as embarrassed as he did.

"Oh, Miss Shaw," said Mrs Partridge, bustling down the slope toward them. "Never say you've been trapped in the icehouse all that time. I'm certain Master Philip didn't know you would be shut up in there for so long—"

"Master Philip?" Evelina said with an edge to her voice. "What makes you think it was Philip who shut me in? I'm sure it was just an accident. A gardener must have seen the door ajar and thought it had been left open by mistake, never realising someone was inside."

"That's very noble of you, Miss Shaw, to try to protect the boy like that. I confess I would not be so ready to forgive such a naughty trick. Why, if he carries on like this unheeded, someone could get hurt."

"Thank you for your concern, Mrs Partridge. I believe that Mr Derringer and I can deal with the situation."

The woman gave an audible sniff. "Very good, madam," she said, and with a toss of her chin in the air, she headed back to the house.

John was alone again with Evelina, but the moment was lost. She hugged her arms around her body, putting up a barrier between them, keeping him at a distance. To judge by the sour expression on her face, she was in no hurry to repeat the kiss. Which was disappointing, as he dearly wanted to repeat it, over and over again. Clearly, he had been as lacking in his kissing as he was in everything else.

CHAPTER 27

*E*velina watched the housekeeper's retreating form until she was out of sight. Bother that woman. Why did every encounter with her leave an unpleasant taste in Evelina's mouth? Mrs Partridge had upset her. She had upset Philip. And now she seemed determined to drive a wedge between John and his nephew.

Without John's arms around her, the chill of the icehouse seeped back into her body. Evelina hugged her arms across her front, trying to stop the cold from sending her into another fit of shivering. She wished John would take her back in his arms and kiss her again like she had been sure he was going to before the wretched Mrs Partridge interrupted them. No one had ever kissed her before—and now it looked as if John would not be tempted to kiss her again.

The tenderness in his eyes had gone, replaced by a sterner, more distant emotion. His expression was serious, dour even, without the slightest upturn to his mouth. Was this really the same man who had just kissed her with considerably more passion than she had deemed possible?

He must regret his sudden show of emotion. She hoped it would not make their relationship more awkward than it was already.

"She's right, you know. It can't have been a mistake," he said.

Evelina inwardly laughed at her own stupidity. John wasn't even thinking about her or the kiss they'd shared.

With an effort, she switched her thoughts back to the housekeeper's poisonous words. "Of course, it could have been a mistake. Mrs Partridge has planted an unfortunate idea in your mind. Why would you believe Philip would act like that when his behaviour has improved so much? Why don't we ask him?"

John huffed. "It won't do any good—if we can even find him. He was not in the schoolroom when I came in search of you. It is the same old pattern emerging—fighting, shutting his governess in and running away. The first sign of opposition and he reacts like this—"

"Opposition? What do you mean?"

"You took something away from him that he wanted —to dig today. He reacted badly."

"I suppose Mrs Partridge told you that."

John gave a curt nod.

Evelina struggled to control her frustration at the woman's interference. "It wasn't like that. Philip accepted his punishment and went up to the schoolroom while I went to fetch ice."

"Then why wasn't he there when I looked?"

Evelina wished for Philip's sake he had done as she asked. "I don't know, but I'm sure there's a good explanation for it."

"I admire your faith in your pupil, Miss Shaw," he said, clipping his words, so they sounded more like an accusation than a conversation, "but it is misplaced. The boy rebelled against having his will crossed and reverted to his old habits."

Evelina smarted to hear John address her in that formal manner. Philip was not the only one to revert to old habits.

"I find that hard to believe," she said.

"And I find it hard to think otherwise. You cannot defend him."

"I shall not continue to defend him if he is guilty, but you are passing judgement without knowing all the facts. I merely wish to know the truth."

"Ah, the truth. Do you think it likely a ten-year-old boy will own up to a piece of mischief that will get him into serious trouble? I've been too soft on the boy."

John's expression remained unyielding. He was not interested in the truth. He had already made up his mind that Philip was to blame.

"When I discovered the schoolroom was empty, I walked down to the river, to the site where we're digging, but there was no sign of him. Let's try the stables. If he has been in one fight today, who's to say he won't get into another?"

John strode in that direction, taking such large paces she had to scurry to keep up. He did not talk, and Evelina made no attempt to break the tense silence between them.

It was a relief to discover Philip was not in the stable yard, engaged in another fight. No one had seen him since she had found him there earlier.

But Evelina had to admit that the evidence was not in

Philip's favour. She was still reluctant to blame him for what had happened without hearing his side of the story, but it seemed indisputable that he had run away to hide. And if he had run away to hide, Evelina thought she knew where they would find him.

"When you went down to the river, did you look under the bridge?" she asked.

"Under the bridge? Why?"

"It was where I first discovered Philip's collection of tesserae. I suspect it is his favourite hiding place."

She led the way down the path to the river and climbed down the bank. At one point, her foot slipped, and John shot out a hand to steady her, but as soon as her feet were back on a firm footing, she snatched her hand back. Now was not the time for intimacy. Indeed, she had not felt so out of charity with John since her very first interview with him.

Evelina made her way along the edge of the river until she reached the bridge. Peering under, she could see the boy, curled up on the stone where she had found his treasures.

"Hello, Philip."

He jumped up. "Miss Shaw. Uncle."

"What are you doing here?" Evelina said. "Why aren't you in the schoolroom as I asked?"

"I did go up there," he said in a small voice, "but I tired of waiting. I went to look for you, but Mrs Partridge saw me and scolded me, telling me I was in big trouble...and so, I ran away and hid."

"Mrs Partridge scolded you for good reason," John said. "Miss Shaw was shut in the icehouse for a long time. It is only by the grace of God she did not fall and hurt herself."

Philip's mouth fell open, and he stared up at her with wide eyes, full of concern. "Is that why you didn't come?"

"Yes," she said. "Someone shut me in by mistake and I would still be there if your uncle hadn't come looking for me."

"It was no mistake," John said. "No one would close the door of the icehouse without first checking it was empty. It is clear to me, if it is not to you, that someone shut you in the icehouse on purpose—and there is only one person I can think of who has a habit of doing things like that."

He glared at Philip. "Well?"

His nephew stared up at him, his expression showing how appalled he was by the suggestion. "I didn't do it."

"Come now. You are only prolonging this by not confessing. I'm sure you didn't mean for Miss Shaw to be shut up in the cold for so long, but—"

"I didn't do it."

"So, you weren't angry about not being allowed to dig today?"

"Yes, I was angry. It wasn't fair. I didn't mean to get into a fight—"

"Ah yes, the fight. Mrs Partridge told me about that. I suppose that is why your face looks so ghastly." John shifted his gaze to Evelina. "Are you still intent on telling me the boy's behaviour has changed? The evidence says otherwise."

"Philip knows it was wrong and has apologised," she said, her temper rising in Philip's defence at the uncompromising tone in John's voice. Why was he determined to think the worst of his nephew—and of her? Because if John thought Philip had not changed, then he was stripping her of all the praise he had lavished on her for the improvement in the boy's behaviour.

"That is something, I suppose, but I fear I have left him unchecked for too long. It is my mistake. I should have put a stop to these bad-tempered outbursts months ago. If they are allowed to continue, someone might get seriously hurt. I find it disturbing that he went looking for a fight and even more disturbing that he locked you in the icehouse."

"I didn't do it," Philip whined, "and I didn't go looking for a fight."

"Yet, you were fighting. Can you deny it?"

"No, sir, but—"

"Or that you were angry Miss Shaw said you couldn't dig today?"

"I told you I was angry, but I was going to do—"

"Can you deny you shut Miss Shaw in the schoolroom the day after she arrived?"

Philip's bottom lip quivered. "No, sir."

"Or that you shut Miss Shaw in the icehouse today?"

"Yes!"

"So, you are a liar, too?"

"No!" Philip shouted, stamping his foot in frustration. "Why won't you believe me?"

"Then why did you run off and hide?"

"Because Mrs Partridge yelled at me. I might have known she would say it was my fault and you would believe her. I shouldn't have hidden—I should have just run away and never come back, because now you'll send me to school just like horrid Mrs Partridge wants and—"

"That is quite enough," John said. "Perhaps Mrs Partridge is right, and I've made a mistake keeping you here, as you clearly do not heed me or your governess. Go up to the schoolroom and write a letter of apology to Miss Shaw, and when you've finished, bring it to my study."

"But I didn't do it," Philip said, an agonised look in his eyes.

"To persist in claiming your innocence will not change my mind. Get out of my sight."

Philip cast a pleading look up at Evelina, but she did not dare oppose John in front of the boy. She gave a tiny shake of her head, and Philip dropped his gaze, as though she had just withdrawn his last pillar of support.

"Run along and do as your uncle says. I will be up soon to see how you are getting on."

Philip's shoulders shook as he clambered up the bank and ran back to the house.

John climbed up after him and offered Evelina his hand, but she refused to take it. She was in no mood to receive help from him. Though she would not argue with John in front of Philip, she had no intention of letting the matter rest.

CHAPTER 28

*E*velina struggled up the bank after John and then walked behind him all the way back to the house, making sure she did not catch him up. With every step, her indignation grew. How could John be so...so pig-headed?

She followed him into his study, and they almost collided as he turned to close the door, not realising she had stalked his footsteps.

"I believe you are in error, Mr Derringer," she said, standing in the open doorway with her hands on her hips.

"And I believe you are overly protective of the boy. You will not stop me sending him to school if I judge that to be the best course of action."

"Why would you do that when you have seen such improvements in his behaviour?"

"I do not call lying an improvement."

"I believe Philip is telling the truth."

"Miss Shaw, you spent over an hour shut up in cold, damp and darkness. You could have fallen and broken your leg or—" He pressed his lips together hard before starting again in a gentler tone. "What if I had not found you when I did? The ice has almost gone. It might have been weeks before anyone had reason to go into the icehouse again."

"Mrs Coombes knew where I was going, as did Philip. I'm sure they would not have left me to rot."

"Why are you still trying to excuse the boy?"

"Philip," Evelina reminded him. "He is not just any boy. He is your nephew, and his name is Philip."

"Have it your way. Why would you still seek to excuse *Philip*? He lost his temper and in a fit of rage, he shut you in the icehouse. When Mrs Partridge accused him, and he thought he had been found out, he ran away and hid."

"The offence was against me. I'm grateful you came looking for me, for it was not a pleasant experience, but no harm was done. If I'm ready to accept Philip's word that he did not shut me in the icehouse, surely that is enough?"

"You're being ridiculous in your efforts to protect him. There is no other explanation."

"Yes, there is. Someone else could have shut me in," she countered.

"You would rather believe that one of my servants shut you in by mistake?"

Evelina shrugged her shoulders. "It seems unlikely, but what other explanation is there?"

"I thought not," John said, a look of triumph on his face. "Your line of reasoning is flawed."

"If I believe Philip is telling the truth, then the other alternative, however unlikely, must have occurred." She could see she was exasperating him, but she refused to back down. "Are you really willing to throw away your better understanding of your nephew over this?"

When John said nothing, she continued in a coaxing tone. "Is it so difficult to take Philip at his word? Could you not give him the benefit of the doubt?"

"Miss Shaw, let us get one thing straight. Philip is—and always will be—my responsibility. As my future wife, you are my responsibility too, and I must act in the way I see fit to protect you both. You are not Philip's mother, or aunt or any other blood relation—you are merely his governess. You have no right to lecture me on how to deal with my own nephew."

The words struck Evelina like a slap in the face, waking her from a lovely dream. How dare he kiss her and give her the hope of something more and then relegate her to being nothing more than an unpleasant duty? She felt as if he had taken her to the top of a mountain and shown her a glimpse of a beautiful view, only to push her over the edge of the cliff.

"Is that what you see me as—a responsibility?" she said, spitting out her words, her volume rising, fuelled by her growing anger. "Well, this 'mere governess' does not want to be a responsibility. If you plan to send Philip to school, you no longer need a governess. There is nothing further for me to do. You may consider our engagement at an end. I would prefer to live out my days in seclusion than become an unwelcome responsibility."

Evelina did not wait for John to answer. She needed to leave the study before her anger faded—before the hurt resurfaced and the depth of her feelings showed. Feelings he did not share. Now, she saw the kiss outside the icehouse in a different light. He saw her as his responsibility—nothing more. She had thrown herself into his arms, and he had comforted her with a kiss. It was mortifying to think she had looked as if she were inviting it.

She stormed out of the room and almost collided with Mrs Partridge. Colour flooded Evelina's face as she hurried past the housekeeper, half-walking, half-running along the corridor. How much of their conversation had that troublemaker overheard? Evelina had not even bothered to shut the door behind her in her haste to confront John. But what did it matter now? She was leaving. Mrs Partridge had got what she wanted.

And Evelina? She had lost everything.

By the time she reached the stairs, the tears were falling down her face. Her reputation would be in ruins —Mrs Franklin would see to that—but it couldn't be helped. Evelina knew she would never recover, anyway. How could you recover when your heart had been broken in two? When they had kissed, she thought she had seen something quite different in his expression, and it was painful to extinguish that glimmer of hope that she was not doomed to a life without love.

Something inside her felt hollow. That tender feeling she had experienced for just a moment had been cruelly gouged out with a knife. She had been wrong about John. The man she had left in the study was not the same man who had rescued her from the icehouse. His harsh words still rang in her ears. She could not reconcile it with the man who had helped her and Philip dig for Roman treasures.

Philip. She felt a pang of pain, deep inside. Poor Philip. He would be sent to school—sent away from the affection his uncle had started to show him. Away from her.

That hurt, too. She cared for Philip far more than just as her pupil. Any hope that she might have become more to Philip than his governess had gone. She shuddered to think of the impact it would have on a boy who was only just reaching out again after the pain of losing his parents.

But she could not stay. Not now. John had made it clear he would not view her as his equal, even in marriage. She was just a responsibility—an unlooked for, unwelcome responsibility.

Despite the mealtimes they had shared. Despite the pleasant afternoons they had spent together, digging away, looking for Roman treasures. Despite the kiss.

No, she could not stay.

CHAPTER 29

*J*ohn sat in his chair, staring at the open doorway. What had he done?

It had all happened so fast. He had been angry from the moment he woke up—infuriated with his own shortcomings. His ill-temper had been simmering so close to the surface that Evelina's obstinate defence of Philip had made it bubble over.

He shuddered as he remembered what he had said to her. She had never been a 'mere governess'—she had always been something more. And now, she was so much dearer—dearer to him than his own life. Why couldn't she understand he was trying to protect her? That he *was* responsible for her wellbeing, whether or not she liked it. At least, he had been. But now she had gone—out of his study and soon out of his life.

John removed his spectacles and rubbed a hand over his weary eyes, trying to ignore the pain gnawing away at his insides. It was better this way. He would probably fail as a husband as he had at everything else.

He would never forget that moment when he heard a

noise from inside the icehouse. His blood had run as cold as the ice inside at the thought of Evelina being trapped in there, undiscovered. What if he hadn't found her? What if her lantern had gone out, and she had tripped and fallen and...

It would have been his fault. His fault, and his alone. Philip would never have persisted in his tricks if he had been firmer with him from the start. John had been so angry with his lot in life he had not given Philip the affection he craved—the boundaries he needed, and the reassurance he yearned for, that he was wanted—loved.

Love. It wasn't a word John used very often. He had thought his feelings did not run that deep—until Evelina came. In a few short weeks, she had shown him the intelligent, affectionate boy that was hurting so much—a hurt that John had the power to ease. As he had opened up to Philip, giving him time and affection, he had sensed a melting of Philip's grief—and his own.

It was Evelina who had brought that change about. She had captured his heart as well as Philip's. And when they had kissed, all his feelings of inadequacy had melted away. He had felt wanted—loved.

But it had been a dream—a fantasy. He didn't deserve to be loved. When Mrs Partridge had pointed out that Philip must have locked Evelina in the icehouse, John's sense of inadequacy had hit him again with full force.

The torrent of emotion had overwhelmed him. He could not fail. Not again. Even though it meant ignoring Evelina's pleas.

Philip needed to own up to what he'd done, and then they could move on. How could he forgive his nephew if he continued to deny the truth? He could not. The boy must be lying—and he would not have a liar in his house.

John did not know how long he sat there, lost in the misery of his reflections, but they were brought to an abrupt halt when the door burst open. Philip stood on the threshold, tears streaming down his face.

"Punish me for shutting Miss Shaw in the icehouse. I was angry. Please bring her back."

John furrowed his brow. "You admit you lied?"

"I take full blame for what happened," he said, a determined look in his eyes. "Beat me if you like, or set me to write a hundred letters of apology, but please don't send Miss Shaw away. It's not her fault."

John let out a heavy sigh. "I didn't send her away, Philip. She's chosen to leave—and I can't make her stay."

He paused. Even in the depths of his misery, John could imagine what Evelina would say. She would coax him to tell Philip the truth if he wanted to encourage the boy to be honest with him.

"I lost my temper, and I said some hurtful things to Miss Shaw that she won't be able to forget. She doesn't want to marry me anymore. She wants to go home."

Philip swiped his hand across his nose and gave a huge sniff. "You could say you are sorry. God will forgive you. Maybe Miss Shaw will too."

John stared at Philip. It sounded so obvious when he said it.

Philip stared back, an intense look in his eyes. "You want her to stay, don't you?"

John did not want to admit how empty he felt at the thought of Evelina going out of his life. Six months ago, he thought he needed no one. Now, he realised that both

Philip and Miss Shaw had become important to him. They were the family he never knew he needed.

"Yes, Philip. I want her to stay."

"Then we must stop her before she leaves."

John didn't move. Was it really that simple? To say he was sorry. To say he wanted her to stay. What if he told her he loved her? Would it make any difference to her decision to leave?

A spark of hope flickered in his heart.

Philip came round the side of John's desk and grabbed him by the hand. "You must come now, or it will be too late."

"I don't think she's leaving today, Philip."

"But she is. The carriage is out the front waiting for her."

"You must be mistaken."

"Come and see."

John let Philip lead him out of the house, but there was no sign of the carriage.

"We're too late," Philip wailed, his face contorted with pain, as he pointed in the distance to where a coach was passing out the gates of the Hall.

The spark of hope in John's heart flickered for a moment and then died.

Evelina had gone.

CHAPTER 30

*E*velina stared out of the window of the carriage, but she saw nothing of what they passed on the road to Bath. All her thoughts lingered on what she had left behind.

When the tears came, her anger had evaporated, and Evelina was filled with remorse. John had hurt her, and she had lost her temper, throwing her betrothal back in his face. She had thought to return to his study to apologise and see if he would forgive her, hoping that he, too, regretted his harsh words. They had both been angry and said things they did not mean.

But John's pride had clearly been hurt too badly. Within minutes of returning to her chamber, she had received a message telling her that the travelling carriage would be ready for her departure within the hour. She had helped Maggie pack, tears streaming down her face. All that remained was an ache deep inside that would gnaw away at her until the day she died.

She had nothing left to say, but Maggie more than made up for it. Evelina let her talk. She was in need of distraction and there was something comforting about listening to her maid chattering away.

"Who would have thought it of such a gentleman as Mr Derringer?" Maggie said. "Throwing us out as if we were the leftovers from yesterday's dinner. And poor Master Philip—he was so fond of you. What will he do without you? That Mrs Partridge will have him shipped off to school in no time. That's what they were saying below stairs when I asked Stevens to get our trunks down. He was mighty sorry to see me go."

She sniffed hard, and Evelina threw her a sympathetic look.

"No matter," Maggie said. "That's the way life goes. Ups and downs. We're on a down just now, but those Partridges are on a real up. They looked mighty pleased to see the back of us. Mayhap they knew if you became mistress of the Hall, they'd be out before you could say Jack Robinson. I know it's not my place to speak ill of those above me, but there's a couple I shan't be sorry to leave behind. That Mrs Partridge is a cold-hearted woman, if ever there was. Polly says she wouldn't visit her father on his deathbed, even though he asked for her—"

"Oh?" said Evelina, turning away from the window, her attention caught at last. It was not that long ago she had overheard Mrs Partridge's threatening words to a man she'd called Father. She rarely encouraged her maid to gossip, but curiosity overcame her scruples. "Did he die recently?"

Maggie tossed her head back and tutted loudly. "Course he did. He was that Mr Bromley that was the steward here afore that nice Mr Walker came."

Evelina's mouth dropped open in surprise. "I didn't realise."

"Suppose I only know because Polly was fond of the old man. She'd known him all her life, long before his wits went a-wandering. Still, that isn't a good reason to refuse your pa's dying wish, is it? Just because he was a mite confused all the time. Poor fellow. I hope I don't lose my wits before I die."

"What did they say of him below stairs—old Mr Bromley, that is?"

Maggie shrugged her shoulders. "Nothing much. Plenty to say about the Partridges, though, when they weren't a-listening. They haven't been at the Hall long. Came when Mr Derringer took over the place from his father, when he got poorly after Master Philip's parents died. Why such a nice man as Mr Derringer would employ—but then again, maybe he's not such a nice man as I thought he was."

"That's enough, Maggie," Evelina said, more sharply than she had intended. "I won't hear you speak against him."

"Never say you're still sweet on him—"

"Maggie! Curb your tongue. I was the one who ended our engagement—"

Evelina broke off as the carriage drew to a halt. Why had they stopped? They couldn't have reached Bath already.

She looked out of the window and saw to her astonishment they had drawn up alongside a carriage coming from the opposite direction.

A moment later, the door was opened by an unfamiliar footman.

"If you please, madam, Mrs Derringer would like you to join her."

She gasped with surprise. John's mother was in the other vehicle? She must be on her way to Duriel Hall.

Evelina hesitated. The last thing she wanted was to face Mrs Derringer. She wanted to run and hide, but it was only delaying the inevitable. His mother would have to be told their engagement was over.

She took a deep breath and allowed the footman to help her move from one carriage to the other, exchanging places with Mrs Derringer's maid.

The older woman's gaze swept over her. Evelina knew her red eyes and worn look had not gone unnoticed when Mrs Derringer's welcoming smile faded, and her brow creased with concern.

She patted the seat next to her. "Come, sit, and tell me what has happened, dear child."

Evelina did as she was bid, lacing her hands together in her lap to stop them from fidgeting.

"I...I..."

Mrs Derringer reached out a hand to pick up a box that lay beside her on the seat. "I was on my way to visit you," she said, holding out the leather case to Evelina, "to give you this."

Without thinking, Evelina took the case in her hands, undid the catch, and pushed open the lid. And then she stared. Inside, resting on a cream velvet lining, was a string of rubies and diamonds, with a large heart-shaped pendant comprising a single ruby. It was the most beautiful necklace she had ever seen.

All at once, she came to her senses and snapped the case shut. Mrs Derringer would not want to give her this now. It must be an engagement present—a breathtakingly gorgeous and valuable engagement present—but alas, she was no longer engaged.

She pushed the case back toward Mrs Derringer. "I'm sorry," she said. "I don't know what I was thinking. This is not for me. I...we...your son and I are no longer betrothed."

Mrs Derringer took the case back and opened it again. She traced the shape of the ruby pendant with her fingers. "It's called the Heart of the Hall. William gave it to me as a symbol of his love. He said it was to remind me I held his heart. I have talked with him, and we agree— the necklace belongs to the woman who holds the heart of the current master of the Hall. And that, my dear, is you."

Evelina shook her head, the tears welling up inside her like a rain cloud threatening an almighty downpour. "I am just a responsibility—an unwelcome responsibility. It was all a lie. We didn't fall in love. John offered for me to save my reputation, though I thought he cared, just a little. But then he wouldn't listen to me, and said the most cutting things. And so I broke off our engagement" —here she let out a sob—"but I was sorry, and I would have tried to put it right, but he sent me away without another word."

"You may think he offered for you out of duty, but I know my son better. Circumstances may have seemed to force his hand, but—bother the man. So like his father. Why has he left you in doubt of his affection?"

Evelina took out a handkerchief from her reticule and blew her nose. Could Mrs Derringer be right? That she had been more to John than an unwelcome responsibility? But what did it matter now? She had ended their engagement. It was too much to expect him to repeat his offer.

While Evelina was lost in her thoughts, Mrs

Derringer seemed to have come to a decision. "I will not ask you to return to the Hall and face John now, Evelina, but don't go back to Bristol just yet. Come and stay with me in Bath. I believe my bad-tempered son is in love with you, but maybe he does not realise it himself. It would be beneficial for him to miss you."

Evelina was too desperate to argue. If there was even a faint hope of a future with John, she was going to try for it. But what of his nephew?

"Philip has no governess, and John is angry because he thinks he's been lying to him. He won't really send him away to school, will he?"

"No. Despite his threats, I'm sure he would not go against his brother's wishes. But what is this? Philip lying? I see you have plenty to tell me on the way back to Bath."

Mrs Derringer rapped her cane on the roof of the carriage. The footman came back to the door.

"Turn the coach around. I wish to return to Bath. Tell Grayson to follow with our maids and Miss Shaw's luggage."

"Very good, madam."

Ten minutes later, Evelina resumed her journey away from Duriel Hall, away from the man she loved. But she no longer felt so despondent. Mrs Derringer's words had rekindled a small flame of hope in her heart that perhaps —despite everything—John might care for her.

CHAPTER 31

*I*t was well into the afternoon when Partridge informed John his carriage had returned. He did not need to be told twice. He raced out of his study to the stables, anger bubbling just below the surface, desperate to find someone—anyone—to blame for aiding Evelina's abrupt departure.

"Perhaps you can explain to me, Grayson, just where you've been."

The coachman, who had known him since he was a boy, gave him a hard stare. "No, sir, I cannot."

John's mouth fell open in surprise. "You can't?"

"Forgive me, sir, but I gave my word."

"Then you took Miss Shaw away?"

"Yes, sir."

"But why, Grayson? Why did you see fit to take my carriage out on her orders?"

"I didn't. It was Mrs Partridge who ordered the carriage to be brought round."

"Mrs Partridge?"

"She said that you and Miss Shaw had had a terrible

argument, and Miss Shaw had declared she would not spend another night under your roof. Told me to get the carriage ready as you would not keep her here against her will. I couldn't imagine Miss Shaw being in such a rush to leave, but I was wrong. So I took her away, supposing I was obeying your orders."

John gritted his teeth. He stormed back into the house and demanded to see Mrs Partridge.

The woman walked into his study ten minutes later, her face a picture of innocence.

"Did you, or did you not, order Grayson to bring my carriage around earlier?"

"I did," said Mrs Partridge.

"By whose authority?"

"Why, Miss Shaw's, of course. She is your affianced wife, so I thought it only right to accept her request. Did I do wrong?"

"You're lying. If you told Grayson we argued, you must have known Miss Shaw had broken off our engagement."

Mrs Partridge failed to repress the glimmer of a smile. That was the last straw.

How could he have been blind for so long? The woman was revelling in the fact that his engagement had ended. She didn't want Evelina in the house any more than she wanted Philip. Time and again she had brought his nephew's misdemeanours to his notice, urging him to send the boy to school. From the moment Evelina had arrived, Mrs Partridge had been set against her— undermining her progress with Philip and ensuring John was aware of every time she failed.

When he had announced his betrothal, the housekeeper's words had unsettled him, making him doubt himself and Evelina. Now he saw those words in a different light. They were designed to push them apart.

It might be too late to get Evelina back, but he would not put up with this woman and her divisive influence in his household. She would have to go.

"I no longer require your services, Mrs Partridge. I want you and your husband out of my house within the week. Mr Walker will pay whatever is owing to you. You are dismissed."

John had the satisfaction of seeing the smile wiped off the woman's face.

"But I was only—"

"No, Mrs Partridge. You were not. One week. You may go."

There was no denying the scowl on the woman's face as she left the room, the veneer of politeness gone without a trace.

John shuddered. If that was the face she had shown Philip, no wonder his nephew disliked the woman so much.

Now he had dismissed his housekeeper, his anger abated, but his hopelessness did not. Sending Mrs Partridge away would not bring Evelina back.

⁓ • ⁓

THE NEXT FEW DAYS DRAGGED. Long, lonely days without Evelina. The house seemed so empty without her. John had treated her abominably, and she had gone, leaving a gaping wound in his heart. Would the pain ever go away? Not only the pain of losing her, but the pain from blaming himself, knowing that if he had acted in a more gentlemanlike way, she would never have left.

John spent several hours each day in the schoolroom. Evelina had wanted him to share his love of history with Philip, and that was what he was doing, to the best of his ability. But giving the boy his attention was not enough. His nephew was quieter than before. The spark seemed to have gone out of him.

He suspected Philip missed Evelina as much as he did. It would not surprise John to learn that his nephew struggled to forgive him for driving Evelina away. He had certainly not forgiven himself.

Why had he ever questioned Philip's word? If he had given him the benefit of the doubt as Evelina had urged, she would still be here, and Philip would not act as if all the joy had been sucked out of him.

It was still impossible for John to believe Philip had not locked Evelina in the icehouse, but what did it matter now? To judge from the boy's subdued behaviour, he had learned his lesson. Evelina had been right. No one had been hurt, and it had not been worth jeopardising his relationship with Philip. John wondered whether the damage he had done could ever be repaired.

He longed to write to Evelina, but what excuse did he have? They were no longer engaged. He could not risk further harm to her reputation by engaging in correspondence. Besides, what was there to say apart from the fact he was sorry, and he doubted sorry would be enough.

Tomorrow was Wednesday, when he and Philip would visit his parents in Bath. He hoped his mother would not blame him for alienating Evelina as much as he blamed himself. Perhaps she could cheer Philip up. Every attempt John made failed.

"Shall we look at the Roman mosaic this afternoon and see if we can finish uncovering it?" John asked, desperately trying to bring a smile to his nephew's lips.

Philip fixed John's face with an accusing stare. "No, thank you, sir. It won't be the same without Miss Shaw."

A lump formed in John's throat.

"Have you...have you told Grandmother and Grandfather that Miss Shaw has gone?"

John shook his head.

"I think they'll be sad. They like her," Philip said, swiping his hand across his eyes to brush away a few tears he was bravely trying to prevent. "I like her too."

"So do I," said John, taking the boy's hand and squeezing it, a wistful smile on his lips as his own eyes threatened to water up. He blinked away the show of weakness, but it seemed to do him no disfavour in his nephew's eyes.

"I know." Philip squeezed his hand back and gave John the first tender look he'd seen in days. "It's like with Mother and Father. It will hurt a lot at first, and then, after a while, it will become bearable. Except that, every now and again, it gets you right here"—he thumped his chest—"and it makes you want them back so badly that it hurts all over again."

"But Miss Shaw isn't dead."

Philip shrugged his shoulders. "It feels the same. She's gone—just like Mother and Father."

John pondered his nephew's words until he wanted to shout out loud. No. It was not the same.

A sliver of excitement wormed its way up inside John as the realisation hit him. How could he have been so stupid? There was nothing he could do to bring Philip's parents back—but Evelina? He had not even tried to get her back. If there was even the slightest chance she would forgive him, shouldn't he at least try? As long as she was alive, there was hope.

He didn't know where Evelina was. Grayson remained firm in his refusal to divulge her location, and John refused to push the man to break his word. His coachman had assured him she was safe with friends in Bath, but was she still there or had she returned to Bristol? How would he find her? He would write to Anne. His sister-in-law would know where she was.

John would go to Evelina and beg her to come back. On his knees, if necessary. For Philip's sake—and for his own.

"We'll find her, Philip, and I will do everything in my power to bring her back—I promise. I will tell her how sorry I am about what I said, and you must pray she will forgive me." He wanted to add his prayer that she would still marry him, but somehow, he could not bring himself to say the words.

"Can you do that?"

Philip nodded, and John felt more at peace than since before Evelina had left.

CHAPTER 32

*J*ohn was keen to put his plan into action without delay. He had already wasted too much time.

"Let's go down to my study, Philip. You can look at some of my Roman finds while I write to your aunt to see if she knows where Miss Shaw has gone."

Philip gave an eager nod and hurried to clear the table. He was returning his books to the shelf when there was a knock, and the door was opened by a footman.

"If you please, sir," said the man, who seemed out of breath, "you're needed downstairs. Mr and Mrs Derringer are waiting for you in the drawing room."

John's jaw went slack. His parents were here? What had brought them to Duriel Hall, unless...Had Anne written to them and told them Evelina had left? Did they have news of her?

John's heart thumped uncomfortably hard at the thought. Any news of Evelina would be welcome.

He dismissed the footman and gave Philip a quick

look over. "You'll do. Let's go and see your grandparents."

They walked downstairs together, but John sent his nephew into the drawing room ahead of him, bracing himself for his mother's disappointment when he told her his engagement was over.

"Hello, Philip."

John froze in the doorway, hardly daring to believe his ears. He would recognise Evelina's voice anywhere. His feet propelled him forward, though his mind was full of questions. How could she be here—with his parents?

"Miss Shaw!" Philip cried, abandoning restraint and running to throw his arms around Evelina.

She laughed as she wrapped her arms around him. John thought her laughter was the most beautiful sound he had ever heard. He watched as she bent over and kissed the top of Philip's head and, if he was not mistaken, there were tears in her eyes, and such tenderness it took his breath away. There was no doubt she loved the boy.

A deep sense of longing threatened to overwhelm him, and he rested his hand on the door handle to steady himself. Delighted as he was that his nephew had received such a warm response, he wished Evelina was enveloping *him* in her embrace and looking at *him* with such affection.

"We thought you'd gone forever," Philip cried. "Please don't go away again. We miss you so much."

John's gaze did not waver from Evelina's face. A warm glow spread over her cheeks as if she knew he was staring at her, but she did not raise her eyes to meet his. She gave all her attention to Philip, who had launched into a detailed account of everything they had done since she had gone.

How long he would have stood there, gawping like a lovesick boy, he did not discover.

"Good morning," Araminta Derringer said to her son.

John dragged his eyes away from Evelina and stepped forward to kiss his mother's cheek.

"I don't understand..." he said.

"Neither do I," his mother replied with an edge to her voice. "Why in heaven's name did you break off your engagement when it is clear you are head over heels in love with her?"

John's mouth dropped open. Was it so very obvious? Did Evelina see it too? No. She had not even looked at him.

"It was her decision—not mine."

"After you told her she was a responsibility."

John winced.

"My dear boy, I have learned in my life that there is always hope where there is love. You must take risks if you are to love well. Now, sort it out with Evelina," his mother said, "and when you have"—she pushed an oblong case into his hand—"give her this."

John did not need to open the box to know what was inside. The Heart of the Hall—the ruby and diamond necklace which his mother had worn on her wedding day. He took the case and put it on the mantelpiece. That his mother had given it to him inspired him with hope. She would only have done so if she believed Evelina would forgive him.

"Come and give me a kiss," John's mother said, beckoning Philip over to her. "Then we'll go for a walk with your grandfather. I want to see this Roman mosaic you've talked so much about."

Philip hesitated. "Can Miss Shaw come too?"

"Maybe later. I think we should leave her to talk to your uncle."

Philip nodded slowly, like a wise old man. "I think so too." He glanced from John to Evelina and skipped out of the room, followed at a more sedate pace by his grandparents.

His mother shot John one last look of encouragement before shutting the door behind her.

He was alone with Evelina. So many questions rushed into his mind. Why had she left the Hall so quickly? And why, of all places, had she ended up here, with his mother? Was she well? Did she miss Philip? Did she miss him?

He pushed through the fog of unanswered questions to take hold of what was most important. His mother had given him a chance—maybe the only chance he would ever have—to put things right. To tell Evelina how he felt. And he would not waste it.

Saying a quick prayer for courage, John looked Evelina in the eyes—eyes that were at last raised to his.

"I'm so sorry for what I said. Please forgive me."

CHAPTER 33

$\mathcal{E}$velina stared into John's deep brown eyes, so like her own, all her uncertainty mirrored in their depths. She had been so afraid of what she might see there. Afraid his mother was wrong. Afraid John didn't care for her as his mother seemed convinced he did.

Yet here he was, begging her to forgive him, fearing she wouldn't. A great wave of emotion washed over her senses and deprived her of speech. Hope flooded her entire being. He would not look at her like that if he didn't care.

When she said nothing, John started to stride up and down the room.

"I know there is no excuse for the way I behaved, but I was beside myself, imagining what could have happened to you, shut in the icehouse."

He stopped pacing and squeezed his eyes shut for a moment, a look of anguish on his face, before looking into her eyes again. "If you had been hurt or—I would never have forgiven myself. I had let you down, along with everyone else. A man should be able to protect his own family, and I failed in that even before we were married. Just like I failed in my responsibilities toward Philip and the estate."

She tentatively reached out a hand and laid it on his arm, desperate to soothe the anguish she heard in his voice. "You are too hard on yourself. You've failed no one."

"Yes, I have," he said, yanking himself away from her touch.

Evelina was taken aback at the bitterness in his voice. "Tell me."

For a moment, he hesitated, as if debating whether or not to explain what was bothering him, but then he let out a long puff of air and, leaning against the wall, he spoke.

"The day after our engagement, when I should have met you for breakfast—"

"Except that Mrs Partridge made sure I got the wrong time."

"Yes. That morning. My new steward told me I was being cheated by Mr Bromley, the man who had faithfully served our family for decades. I was so angry. Not so much about the money, but that the man had been disloyal to me, and because of my negligence, his crime had gone unnoticed."

Evelina gasped. "I'm so sorry. That must have been hard to accept."

"I didn't want to believe it, but there was no other explanation. I couldn't sleep that night, weighed down by my own inadequacy."

"Oh, John. You're too ready to blame yourself for everything that goes wrong, and the guilt is crushing you.

Is that why you pushed me away? Did you convince yourself you had failed me and that I would be better off without you?"

He grimaced and nodded.

"No wonder you were in such a bad mood that morning. May I ask how Mr Bromley cheated you?"

"He duplicated several names in the wages list and pocketed the money himself."

Evelina remembered what her maid had said to her about Mr Bromley being confused in the months before he died. She screwed up her forehead as she thought about it. Something didn't feel right. "Do you really think he was capable of it?"

"Why would you doubt it?"

"It's something my maid said to me. One of your servants, Polly, was fond of Mr Bromley and told her how muddled the old man became in his last months. That he might write the names out twice by mistake, I can believe, but steal the money? Why would he, when he knew his health was failing, and he had not long for this world?"

John rubbed his chin. "I suppose he was somewhat incoherent during our last few conversations. It would be a comfort to know he was not deliberately trying to defraud me, but who else could have taken the money?"

The question pulled a memory to the surface of Evelina's mind. The conversation she had overheard between Mrs Partridge and her father. Mr Bromley had wailed that he thought his daughter was helping him, and she had told him to be quiet. Could this be what they'd been talking about?

"His daughter," said Evelina with sudden conviction.

"He had a daughter?"

"Yes. Mrs Partridge."

"What? Mrs Partridge was Bromley's daughter?"

"Didn't you realise?"

"No. I knew he had a daughter who went into service after his wife died, but that was when I was a lad. Bromley never thought to tell me they were related when he took the Partridges on."

"I'm sorry. I know you hold your housekeeper in high esteem but—"

"Not anymore."

Evelina raised her eyebrows. "You don't?"

"No. If it wasn't for Mrs Partridge, we might have had this conversation on the day you left, instead of now. I regretted my words as soon as they left my mouth, but I couldn't take them back. When you broke off our engagement, I knew I deserved it. I hoped you would change your mind, but I didn't think my apology would be enough. It was Philip who made me see sense. He came to me in floods of tears and told me he took full blame for shutting you in the icehouse and begged me to ask you to stay—"

"Are those the words he used?"

"Yes, I think so. Does it matter?"

Evelina hesitated, nervous to touch on the subject that had caused their argument. "I believe it confirms what I thought all along. Philip was telling the truth. He didn't shut me in the icehouse, but he was willing to be punished for something he didn't do if it made me stay."

John gave a curt nod. "I hear what you're saying, but I still struggle to believe in his innocence."

"Until a few moments ago, you believed Mr Bromley must have cheated you," Evelina said gently. "That there was no other explanation."

"I see your point. I will try to be open minded about it. Now, where was I? I told Philip I'd hurt you, and he urged me to ask your forgiveness. I came after you, to try to put things right—but I was too late. You'd gone."

"Perhaps if you had not acted so precipitately and thrown me out of your house—"

"But I didn't send you away. It was Mrs Partridge who ordered the carriage, telling the coachman we had argued, and that you refused to spend another night under my roof."

Evelina pulled a face. "That doesn't surprise me. It appears she overheard our argument and was excessively keen to prevent a reconciliation. What a vile thing to do, to send me away like that and make me think it was you."

"After you left, Mrs Partridge made the mistake of revealing her true colours to me. I dismissed her and her husband on the spot. They should be gone in the next few days."

"I'm so pleased. Philip will be much happier without her around. But what of the fraud? Do you intend to confront your housekeeper before she goes, to find out if we're right?"

"I don't know, and I'm not sure I care just now." He took both Evelina's hands in his and drew her toward him. "What I care about, Evelina, is whether you'll forgive me. I know I don't deserve it but—"

She pulled one hand free from his grasp and placed a finger across his lips.

John kissed her finger, sending a delicious shiver down her spine.

He reclaimed her hand and held it in his own, but his tense expression did not disappear.

"Can you...will you..." John grimaced as if a wave of

pain had passed through him. "It was agony thinking I might have lost you in the icehouse, but it was all forgotten when I found you, and you melted in my arms as if you'd come home. I wanted to tell you then how much I loved you and how my heart would have broken if—But you were safe, and when we kissed, I thought you knew…"

Tears sprung to Evelina's eyes as she absorbed those precious words. He loved her.

"These past few days have been worse—much worse. I feel as though I've been wandering around in an endless maze, with no way out. Knowing you were out there, somewhere, hating me—"

"I don't hate you, John. I love you."

A wide smile spread over his face until it lit up his eyes.

"Marry me. Not to be Philip's mother—though I am sure you'll be incredibly good at it—but to be my wife. Not because you have to, in order to save your reputation, but because you want to. Because you love me."

All the tension of the past week melted away. She was not an unwanted responsibility. It wasn't all about Philip. John wanted her. Needed her. Loved her.

"Yes."

"You forgive me, or you'll marry me?"

"Both."

CHAPTER 34

*A*t once, John stood taller. He felt as if a heavy load had been lifted from his shoulders. He reached out his right hand to cup Evelina's cheek, and she nuzzled against his hand as he held it there.

"I thought I'd lost any hope of making you believe I loved you and wanted to marry you because...because I wanted to, and not because I had to. Forgive me. I should not have delayed so long to ask you the first time, but I was a coward. I was afraid you would say no."

Evelina shook her head at him, an exasperated look on her face. "Why would you think that? When you have so much to offer."

"I couldn't forget what you said to me the first time we met. That you would not marry a man simply to become a mother to his children. I thought we were beyond that, but then—when we were first engaged— Mrs Partridge hinted I had trapped you into marrying me. It was when I started to dislike the woman as much as you did."

"She accused me of tricking you, too. What a poisonous tongue that woman has. I'll be glad when she's left the house."

"As will I."

John walked across to the mantelpiece and retrieved the box his mother had given him.

"Mother wanted you to have this," he said, handing it to Evelina. "I think she knew."

Evelina flipped open the lid and gazed at the necklace inside. She traced the shape of the ruby heart pendant with her forefinger and then looked up into his eyes.

"Thank you," she said, her voice filled with awe. "Not just for the necklace, but for what it means. That I hold your heart, as you hold mine."

"In a moment, I will fasten it around your beautiful neck, but first—"

He took off his spectacles and laid them on the nearest table before drawing Evelina toward him and engulfing her in his arms. He kissed her on the forehead, and then lifted her chin, so he could see right into her eyes. The love, the trust he saw there, made his heart swell with joy.

John gulped hard. He would ride to the bishop's office in Wells in the morning to get a marriage licence. There was no way under heaven he could wait for the banns to be read before making Evelina his wife.

He lowered his mouth to hers, but before their lips met, the door opened.

John stepped back, growling in frustration, as Stevens walked into the room. The man must have seen how close his master had been standing to Evelina, but not by so much as the flicker of an eyelid did he betray it.

Despite his annoyance at being interrupted, John had to admit Mr Walker had been right to recommend Stevens as Partridge's replacement. The impassive mask covering the man's features was worthy of his new role as butler.

"Miss Lane is here to see you, sir."

John grabbed his glasses and rammed them back onto his face, trying not to let his irritation show. He cast Evelina a look filled with intense longing. It was some consolation that she appeared to feel the loss as keenly as he did.

"Miss Lane is my—I mean, our—new housekeeper," he said by way of explanation. "At least, I hope so. She's engaged to marry our steward. Though she's not very experienced, I'm confident Walker would not have recommended her if he did not think she was up to the job."

Evelina's eyes twinkled. "I think any housekeeper would be an improvement on Mrs Partridge," she said with a grin.

"Would you like to interview Miss Lane? After all, she will report to you, as mistress of this house."

Evelina blushed a becoming shade of pink. "It might not be what I would choose to be doing just now," she said, biting on her bottom lip and casting him such a look that he felt tempted to kiss her there and then, even under the interested gaze of Stevens. "But as the future mistress of this house, I would be delighted."

John took Evelina's arm and tucked it within his own, squeezing it tenderly as they made their way to the steward's room, where Mr Walker and Miss Lane waited for them.

Once the introductions had been made, John turned to his steward. "I think we can leave the ladies to become acquainted. Please come with me. There is something I need to discuss with you—in private."

Mr Walker gave his betrothed an encouraging nod before following John out of the room.

As soon as they were shut in his study, John shared Evelina's theory about the fraud. "What do you think? Could Mrs Partridge have stolen the money rather than her father?"

The estate manager rubbed his chin. "There is no doubt Bromley was not very coherent on the two occasions I met him, but I put it down to his reluctance to help the man hired to replace him, and thought nothing of it. That Mrs Partridge is Bromley's daughter is—unsettling. And you knew nothing of the relationship?"

"No. I confess, to my shame, I left the appointment of a housekeeper and butler to Mr Bromley. Apart from their personal servants, they were the only staff my parents took with them to their new house in Bath."

"Hmm. No offence to your...intended—"

John could not keep the smile off his face. "Yes. My intended. I am happy to say our differences have been resolved and we are to be wed after all."

"Congratulations, sir. Miss Shaw is an admirable lady."

"Yes, she is, isn't she?"

John stared into space, dwelling on Evelina's excellent qualities, until Mr Walker brought him back to the present with a deliberate clearing of his throat.

"As I was saying, your intended has put substantial weight on the words of her servant, relaying the words of another servant. It would be wise to talk to the young person herself."

"An excellent idea," said John. "I'll send for Polly now."

A nervous rap at the door heralded the maid's arrival a short while later.

"It's all right," John said. "You've done nothing wrong. Please sit down."

Polly perched on the edge of the chair in front of John's desk, and waited, her wide eyes showing how scared she was despite John's reassurances.

"I understand you were fond of my previous steward, Mr Bromley," John said in a gentle voice.

Polly nodded.

"Are you also fond of Mr Bromley's daughter, Mrs Partridge?"

Her eyes grew even larger, and her bottom lip trembled.

"I take it from your silence you are not. You need not be afraid, Polly. I have dismissed Mrs Partridge. She's leaving, and Miss Shaw is even now talking to the lady who will take over from her."

A smile transformed the maid's face. "Then it's true, though Mrs Partridge denied it. That is good news, sir. Mr Bromley would have been so glad."

John blinked. "I beg your pardon. He would have been glad I dismissed his daughter? But it was he who appointed her."

Now her fear of reprisal from Mrs Partridge had been removed, Polly's words flowed freely. "He regretted it. In his last few weeks, he was...unsettled. He mumbled over and over that he never should have brought her here. That he should have known she wouldn't help him. That she would be trouble. He didn't use her name, but I knew who he meant."

There were tears in Polly's eyes. "Made my blood run cold to think she would not stand by her own pa when he was so confused. It wasn't his fault."

"I believe you're right."

After thanking and dismissing Polly, John turned to Mr Walker. "Has she convinced you that Mrs Partridge was manipulating her father for her own ends? The poor man must have seen his reason slipping away and in desperation brought in his daughter to help him keep his job. No wonder he was tortured if in moments of lucidity he realised what she was doing. The risk to her was minimal, as it was her father's handwriting in the ledgers, not hers. How despicable."

"Will you prosecute?"

John let out a long puff of air. "I don't know. It would be tough to prove, and even if it could be done, the law is...harsh. It is a weighty decision to make when it could end a person's life."

Mr Walker nodded. "It is indeed."

"But if there was a way to retrieve what is rightfully mine..."

One thing John liked about Mr Walker was his quick understanding. He grasped the urgency of the situation without him needing to say more.

The man leapt from his chair and moved toward the door ahead of his employer. "I'll have their bedchambers and the housekeeper's room searched now. If there's a hoard of coins hidden somewhere, we'll find it."

John was not hopeful of discovering the stolen money, but he thought it worth the search. There was nothing for him to do but wait, to see if Walker found anything. He strolled along the corridor to the drawing room to discover if his parents had returned from their walk around the grounds.

Perhaps he would find Evelina there instead. His feet sped up at the possibility. Because if he could engineer a few moments alone with her, he'd be able to claim that kiss.

CHAPTER 35

*E*velina sat at the desk in the steward's office with Miss Lane opposite her. She still clutched the case containing the precious jewellery John had given her. The necklace was beautiful, but the love it represented was even more precious.

So much had happened since she had arrived at Duriel Hall that morning. How her world had been turned upside down. She would relive that scene over and over again. John's apology. His declaration of love. The gift of the necklace. And the kiss... She inhaled sharply. The kiss was still waiting for her.

Evelina looked down at the box in her hands. Thank goodness John had not put the necklace around her neck before they were interrupted. It would have been unseemly to flaunt such wealth before a prospective member of staff. She put aside the box, and with it, her thoughts of John—as much as she could.

Evelina looked across the desk at Miss Lane and liked what she saw. Despite being no older than she was herself, the woman seemed self-assured and did not lower her eyes, meeting her gaze straight on. She seemed to be assessing her prospective employer in much the same way that Evelina was assessing her.

"My only housekeeping experience is in my brother-in-law's home, but I make no apology for that." Miss Lane gave a wry smile. "In my opinion, it is harder to work for relatives than anyone else."

Evelina was inclined to agree, as she had learned to be a governess in a similar situation.

After half an hour's conversation, she was convinced of two things—that Miss Lane would likely make an excellent housekeeper, and that, even if she proved less efficient, Evelina would infinitely prefer her to Mrs Partridge.

"How soon can you leave your current position?" she asked.

"Just as soon as you wish," Miss Lane said. "I'm not paid to be the housekeeper, so I fail to see why I need to give notice. No doubt my sister will get over the shock of her younger sister carving her own path in life."

Yes. Evelina liked Miss Lane very much.

"There is, however, one matter to resolve before you start," she said. "The matter of your marriage. I think it best if you wed your Mr Walker before you begin. Mrs Walker sounds a much more respectable name for a housekeeper, don't you think?"

"I do indeed," said Miss Lane, her eyes crinkling at the corners as her smile spread.

"I have to ask—what have you been waiting for?"

Miss Lane met Evelina's inquisitive look without flinching. "I have no dowry, Miss Shaw."

Evelina laughed. "In that, we are alike."

"But Mr Derringer is in a position to support you. I

did not wish to prevent Mr Walker from making his way in the world because of me. Few positions welcome the addition of a wife, Miss Shaw."

"Then I am even more pleased to offer you the role of housekeeper, to enable you to marry without being a burden to your husband. As soon as you are married, you may take up your role. I shall enjoy having you here, Miss Lane."

Without warning, the door burst open, and Mrs Partridge strolled into the steward's office as if she owned it. She started, clearly not realising it was in use. Unabashed, she closed the door behind her and stood with her hands on her hips as she slowly surveyed the room. A smug smile appeared on her lips as her eyes lingered on the desk and then dropped to the rug in front of it.

"What are you doing in here?" Evelina asked. "This is not your office, or even that of your father now."

The malice in the woman's eyes as she raised them to meet Evelina's was almost tangible.

"I repeat, what are you doing in here?"

Mrs Partridge flared her nostrils and looked down her nose at her. "I don't have to answer your questions, Miss Shaw," she said in a far from deferential tone. "You're not mistress of this house yet."

She cast a derogatory glance at Miss Lane. "I suppose this is my replacement—a girl barely out of the schoolroom. I should be careful, Miss Shaw, or you might find your husband's eye wandering with such an attractive alternative on hand."

Evelina was so surprised at the direct attack she was lost for words, but it did not prevent a deep flush from flooding her cheeks at the woman's insinuations.

Miss Lane's colour was also heightened. She jumped up from her chair and faced Mrs Partridge. "How dare you talk to me like that? I am a respectable woman—a clergyman's daughter and engaged to be married—and I will not stand for such insults. You should leave."

Miss Lane moved toward the door and opened it to show the intruder out. Mrs Partridge let out a bark of laughter. "Oh dear. Then you'll be all the more outraged if you come to work here. There is no telling what Mr Derringer did to persuade Miss Shaw to stay. He must have behaved scandalously for her to resume her engagement after such an argument..."

Evelina's mouth fell open in dismay at Mrs Partridge's words. How dare the woman tear John's character to shreds? She threw an apologetic look at her new housekeeper, hoping the young woman was not too shocked. She need not have worried. Miss Lane glared at the older woman, making no attempt to hide her disgust.

"Get out," Evelina said to Mrs Partridge. "You will not get a reference from Mr Derringer after speaking to me in such a manner."

"I think it's too late for that," the woman said, shaking her head from side to side.

"Are you out of your mind?" Evelina asked.

"No. Merely out of options. Your meddling has made Mr Walker ask too many questions. And unlike my father, he knows when two plus two doesn't equal four."

"I thought my dislike of you was distorting my reasoning, but now I see I was right. You stole Mr Derringer's money and left your father to take the blame if you were caught, didn't you? How could you treat your father like that, playing on his confusion and dishonouring his name?"

Mrs Partridge's lip curled in disdain. She made no attempt to refute Evelina's accusation. "For once in his life, the old man was useful to me. He was too confused to preach at me anymore. Ha! He thought I was helping him, but all along, he was helping me. What a triumph to tarnish his reputation when he could do nothing about it. I finally had revenge on him for a lifetime of moralising talk.

"From the moment you arrived, I knew you were trouble. If you had just been like all the others, none of this unpleasantness would have been necessary. You would have left, the child would have been sent away to school, and we might have carried on serving Mr Derringer for years. But you had to change things, didn't you? You couldn't keep your claws out of him. It was a stroke of pure genius to lock you in the icehouse—"

"That was you!" Evelina exclaimed. "I always knew Philip was innocent."

"But Mr Derringer didn't, did he? You can imagine my delight when I heard you arguing. All I had to do was get you out of the house before you could make it up, and everything would go back to the way it was before you came. I should have guessed you would forgive him. You're just like my old man. Perhaps that is why I always disliked you so much."

Evelina was taken aback at the venom in the woman's voice.

"That is quite enough, Mrs Partridge. I suggest you leave—this office, and this house—before I call the constable."

The woman dropped her eyes to the rug in front of the desk again and gave a sinister chuckle. After casting a last look of loathing at Evelina, she strode out of the room.

Miss Lane shut the door behind her. "Well! If that is anything to go by, I think replacing your housekeeper is long overdue."

Evelina stared at the woman as her words hung in the air. The corners of her mouth curled up, mirroring the growing smile on Miss Lane's face. And then, unable to contain themselves any longer, the two women burst out laughing.

When Evelina's mirth had subsided, the gravity of Mrs Partridge's words came back to her. The woman would not dare stay any longer after admitting her guilt. No. If they were to have any chance of retrieving the money she had stolen, they must act now.

She should find John. He would know what to do.

CHAPTER 36

John sat on his own in the drawing room, crossing and uncrossing his legs. He waited for what seemed like an age, hoping Evelina would return before his parents, so they might have some time alone together before they were interrupted again.

How long did it take to interview a housekeeper? She must have finished by now. He would go to the steward's office to find her.

He pulled open the door of the drawing room and almost collided with Evelina.

"Thank goodness I've found you at last," she said.

A glance at her face told him all was not well. "What is it?"

"We were right, John. Mrs Partridge is to blame, not her father. That awful woman barged into the steward's office while I was interviewing Miss Lane and spewed abuse at us both. She admitted it all—even shutting me in the icehouse and pointing the blame at Philip."

John furrowed his brow, a note of resignation in his voice. "So, I was wrong again. I owe Philip an apology for not believing him." He put a protective arm around Evelina's shoulders. "I'm sorry you had to endure that. I should have got rid of her earlier. If she's no longer hiding her crime, she must be certain we won't be able to convict her."

"I think she's about to make a run for it," said Evelina. "I threatened to call the constable. If you want a chance at getting your money back, you need to act fast."

"Mr Walker is already searching their rooms, but I don't think he'll find anything. If the money was found there, we would have the proof we needed. It would be much safer for her to hide it somewhere else until she was ready to leave."

"But where—"

"The steward's office!" John said. "She could have hidden the money there while her father worked here. If anyone found it, he would have taken the blame, not her."

Evelina raised a hand to her mouth and gasped. "Maybe that was why she burst in on my interview with Miss Lane. She had come to retrieve the money."

John grabbed Evelina's hand, and they hurried along the corridor and down the stairs to the steward's office.

The door stood half-open, and John knew he was too late. The rug in front of the desk had been pulled away, and a floorboard prised up. They had found her hiding place. It was empty. Mrs Partridge had retrieved the money and fled.

"Find out whether anyone has seen her leaving," John said. "I'll check the stables."

He half-ran, half-walked all the way there. The sight that reached his eyes was not what he expected. Mr Partridge was slumped against a straw bale in a corner of the yard, imbibing freely from a bottle, while John's stable manager talked to the man in agitated tones.

"But the gig is not safe, I'm telling you. There'll be an accident. I'll lend you a horse to go after her."

Mr Partridge let out a coarse laugh. "What? Are you joking me? With any luck, she'll be killed and then I'll be a free man again."

The stable manager shook his head in amazement. "Don't you care—?"

"Nope. I'm not going to the gallows for the stupid wench—"

"The gallows, Partridge?" John said, breaking in on their conversation.

The man looked up, his focus wobbly. "She nabbed your necklace and thought I'd thank her for it. As I said, stupid wench."

John leaned heavily against the yard wall. Surely the man must be mistaken. He'd been about to put the necklace around Evelina's neck just a short while ago. But her lips had distracted him. And then—they'd been interrupted. What had he done with it? He couldn't remember. It was so difficult to focus on anything with Evelina around.

Had he really been so foolish as to leave the necklace where anyone could pick it up?

John pursed his lips. He wouldn't chase after Mrs Partridge for the money, but the necklace was another matter.

"When did she leave?" he asked.

"No more than half an hour ago."

"Saddle my horse. Now." A groom leapt into action.

John turned to the stable manager. "Take a horse and ride south. I'll go north. I reckon it's most likely she'll head for the city where she can board a stagecoach. If we don't catch her before Bath..."

He mounted his horse and was riding past the front of the house when Walker stepped out the front door.

"I've changed my mind," John called to him. "Send for the constable. I will most definitely prosecute. If I don't catch her now, I will hire all the Runners in Bow Street until I've hunted her down. That wretched woman has stolen the Heart of the Hall."

CHAPTER 37

*D*espite her instructions, Evelina stood in the steward's office, unable to move. She stared at the desk where she had sat a short while before and felt all the colour drain from her face as she realised the box containing the necklace was not there.

Mrs Partridge must have spotted it when she had come into the room earlier. The woman was no fool. She would have recognised the box for what it was—a jewellery case—but she could not have guessed at what was inside. Because of Evelina's carelessness, Mrs Partridge had helped herself to a prize worth far more than the rest.

A cloak of wretchedness descended upon Evelina. How could John ever forgive her for failing to look after the Heart of the Hall? She prayed she would not lose his heart as well.

In a daze, she made her way up to the drawing room. Philip was playing a game of jackstraws with his grandparents.

As soon as Mrs Derringer saw her, she abandoned the game and rushed to her side. "Where's John?"

"I don't know," Evelina said, in a voice devoid of all emotion.

The older woman put a motherly arm around her and rang for some tea. "There is no need to say anything. Just sit. In a while, I will pour you a nice cup of tea. A cup of tea always makes things better."

Evelina did as she was bid and said nothing. Her thoughts swirled around in her head, buffeting against her emotions, making her feel nauseous. Would Mrs Derringer treat her so kindly if she knew her precious necklace had been stolen through her carelessness? More importantly, would John?

The tea arrived, and she sipped it slowly, her eyes glancing to the door at every noise, wondering where John was and when he would return. The wait was torturous. If he couldn't forgive her, she would rather know at once, and leave.

At last, the door opened, and John walked in.

"John," his mother exclaimed. "Come here at once and explain yourself."

But he just stood there, a few steps inside the room, his eyes not meeting Evelina's. He looked so tired, so drawn, she felt compelled to go to him. Taking his hand, she looked up into his eyes.

"I'm so sorry," he said, covering her hand with both of his own. "I didn't catch her in time, but I'll find her, even if I have to hire all the Runners—"

"Will someone please explain what is going on?" the older Mr Derringer asked.

John's mother looked from Evelina to John and back again and shook her head. "When Evelina entered the room half an hour ago, looking as white as a sheet, I thought you had failed to make up with each other. But clearly"—she nodded toward their joined hands—"that is not the case."

"It is the Heart of the Hall, Mother. Our swindling housekeeper stole it as a parting gesture after I dismissed her. It is all my fault. If I had not been so distracted—"

"What are you talking about?" Evelina asked. "It is not your fault, but mine. I laid the box down on the desk in the steward's office when I was interviewing Miss Lane, and in my haste to tell you what Mrs Partridge had said, I forgot about it. It is my fault she had the chance to steal the necklace. Can you ever forgive me?"

"Of course I forgive you, my love," John said, raising Evelina's hand to his lips and pressing a kiss onto her fingers. "You are worth far more to me than rubies."

His words washed away the irrational fear that John would not be able to forgive her carelessness, even as her fingers tingled under his touch. She wondered how she could have doubted him, and was sorely tempted to claim the kiss she had been waiting for all day.

Until she realised three pairs of interested eyes were watching them.

Mrs Derringer was the first to speak. "I'm sorry to hear the necklace is gone, but neither of you is to blame. The thief alone is guilty. And John is right. People are more precious than rubies. Love is of far more value than diamonds. I would give all I possess to have Robert back. When you have loved and lost, you discover what is truly valuable in life."

Philip walked across the room and tugged on John's jacket. "Does that mean Miss Shaw is going to be my aunt, after all?"

John nodded.

"I knew she would forgive you," Philip said, beaming from ear to ear.

———— • ————

THROUGHOUT DINNER, Evelina was aware of John's eyes on her.

"I don't suppose I can persuade you to return to Bath with us," John's mother asked.

The thought of having to leave again so soon was too much for Evelina. "Thank you, but no. My place is here. Isn't that right, Philip?"

"You can't take her away, Grandmother," the boy said, nodding vigorously. "She's only just come home again."

"I thought as much. I sent Grayson to fetch our things. We will stay to lend you a modicum of respectability until you are wed."

"Quite wasted on us," John said, flashing Evelina a grin, "but you are, as ever, most welcome to stay."

"Hmm. Do not encourage your father to linger over his port. The doctor says—"

"Have no fear, Mother. We will join you directly."

John was true to his word. Less than half an hour later, the gentleman joined them in the drawing room. Evelina doubted whether the older Mr Derringer would have had time to drink even a single glass of port in a leisurely manner before his son had whisked him away.

At Mrs Derringer's insistence, Evelina poured the tea and coffee. It was as if she were mistress of the Hall already.

John headed straight to her side. She poured his coffee, aware of his gaze upon her as she added the generous quantity of cream she knew he liked.

As she handed him the cup, her hand brushed his fingers. A tingling sensation shot up her arm, almost making her spill his coffee. The glowing look he gave her suggested he was as conscious of the touch as she was.

"You look entirely too kissable for my peace of mind," he whispered.

She bit down on her bottom lip, the heat rushing to her cheeks at what she saw, simmering in the depth of his eyes.

John's father came up behind him, chuckling, and the moment was gone. "Ah—young love," he said, resting a hand on his son's shoulder.

Evelina turned her attention back to the coffee pot and poured Mr Derringer a cup.

John didn't seem able to drag his eyes away from her until his mother started addressing him.

"When is the wedding?" she asked.

Evelina poured herself a cup of tea, but all her attention was fixed on John. He seemed to have difficulty taking in his mother's words. Perhaps he was still thinking how kissable she looked.

"I...I..."

"The wedding, John. When is it to be?"

Evelina waited with bated breath for his next words. He hoped John would not make her wait too long.

"I thought Saturday."

"An excellent plan," she said, moving to John's side. She was so close to him, she could feel his warmth. It fuelled her impatience for the kiss she had been deprived of earlier. Perhaps she could gain them some privacy without waiting for their guests to retire.

"We must send word to my sister and your brother," she said, trying to keep her tone even. "Do you think we should write those letters now, given that time is so short?"

"Yes, indeed," John said. "Please excuse us, Mother."

They left the room together and, as soon as the door shut behind them, John took her hand in his, apparently not caring what the servants thought. He led her along the corridor in silence. No words were needed. Their joined hands symbolised the emotional bond between them.

Evelina's breath came faster as the anticipation built. Just a few more moments, and they would be alone, and John could claim the kiss she was waiting for.

CHAPTER 38

*J*ohn could hardly believe that Evelina—his Evelina—had been so bold as to suggest they leave the drawing room at once to write letters to their siblings. He hoped she was dwelling as little on those letters as he was. All he could think about was kissing the woman who had agreed to be his wife.

"Excuse me, sir."

Botheration. His new butler seemed intent on waylaying him.

"Yes?"

"The constable is here to see you. I've put him in the library."

John sighed with frustration. He would have to see him, having sent for the man. He had not expected him to come so promptly. Not that he held out much hope of the constable finding the necklace. John knew he would have to hire a Bow Street Runner to have any real chance of retrieving it.

"Thank you, Stevens. I'll join him shortly."

John waited for the butler to leave before turning to Evelina.

"I'm sorry. It seems as if the *letter writing* will have to be delayed."

She nodded. "I had better return to the drawing room until you've finished."

Before he realised what she was about, Evelina leaned forward and kissed his cheek, and then, with a big grin on her face, she headed back along the corridor toward the drawing room.

Half-way along, she paused and glanced over her shoulder. She shot John such a wicked smile that he almost forgot what he was supposed to be doing and ran after her. She must have read his intention and her cheeks turned pink, whether at her own daring in provoking him, or his reaction, he wasn't sure.

He ached to pull her into his arms, but he knew the constable was waiting and let her go.

John found the man pacing up and down the library. He shook his hand and invited him to sit.

"I'd prefer to stand, if you don't mind, sir," the constable said. "The thing is, I've never had to deal with anything like this before."

John tried to reassure him. "I know the necklace is valuable, but in many ways, it's no different to a scullery maid running off with a few candlesticks."

The man screwed up his face in confusion. "I'm not sure I follow you, sir. I'm not talking about stolen property."

"Then you haven't come in response to my steward's message?" John asked.

"No. I've come because there's been an accident, and

the rector says as how the woman was housekeeper here at Duriel Hall—a Mrs Partridge."

John's eyes lit up. "You've found her? That is good news. I dismissed the woman from my service a few days ago, and as her parting act, she stole a necklace—a valuable necklace—from my betrothed. It is, I suppose, what you would call a family heirloom. I am most eager to have it back. I hope you've not let her get away."

"No need to worry about that," the man said in a flat voice. "She was killed outright when a wheel came off the gig and it tipped right over."

"Oh!" John said, dropping into the nearest chair. "That is swift justice indeed." It was a sorry end to a sorry tale of disloyalty and deceit. Maybe it was merciful it had ended this way.

For though John might have let the theft of the money go unpunished, he would not have let go of the necklace so easily. He would have pursued her relentlessly and brought her to justice. "The necklace? Was it on her person?"

"Would you care to describe it to me, sir? Just so as I can be sure it belongs to you. Since it is, as you say, rather valuable."

John rose from his seat and walked over to the portrait of his parents that hung over the fireplace. It had been painted just after their wedding, and around his mother's neck hung the Heart of the Hall.

"Like that," he said, pointing at the ruby and diamond necklace in the portrait. "Exactly, like that."

The man nodded. "It's definitely the same necklace." He reached inside his jacket, pulled out a pouch, and handed it to John. "Yours, I believe."

"Actually, it belongs to my future wife"—he let out a

satisfied sigh as he withdrew the necklace from the pouch —"and she will be delighted to have it restored to her."

"Would you happen to be missing anything else, sir?"

"Money. Quite a lot of it."

"Aha," said the constable, pulling out another pouch and handing it to John. "I thought it was too much for a housekeeper to have on her person."

The second pouch was heavier than the first, and John discovered it was full of coins.

"Thank you. I am most grateful," he said and moved toward the door.

"But what am I to do with the poor woman's body?"

"I believe you should inform her husband and leave him to decide." John rang the bell, and Stevens reappeared.

"Is Mr Partridge still on the premises?" he asked.

"Yes, sir."

"Please, could you bring him to see the constable? Prepare him for sad news, if you can. His wife has been killed in an accident."

With a quick nod, the butler disappeared. Within minutes, he returned with Mr Partridge in tow.

"I will leave you in Stevens's capable hands," John said, hurrying out the door, so he did not have to witness Partridge's unholy delight at being told he was a widower.

John closed the door behind him, shutting out all thoughts except one. He hurried back to the drawing room with that one thought in his mind. Kissing Evelina.

JOHN'S PARENTS RETIRED EARLY, not long after Philip, leaving Evelina alone in the drawing room. She tried to read, but she knew it was a pretence. The book lay open on her lap unread as she thought over the events of the day, waiting for John to return.

The minutes dragged, but at last the door opened. It was John. She leapt to her feet, sending the book clattering to the floor.

Without a word, he walked across the room to where she was standing, a crooked smile on his lips. He had two drawstring bags in his hands. One he placed on a table. The other he opened. Evelina gasped as he pulled out the missing necklace.

"I would willingly trade a dozen ruby necklaces to have you as my wife," he said, fastening it around her neck, "but this heart—and mine—truly belongs to you. It's good to have you both safely home at the Hall."

Evelina gave him a shy smile as she raised her eyes to meet his. "It is good to be home."

For the second time that day, John took off his spectacles and laid them aside before pulling her close, engulfing her in his embrace. He covered her face with kisses, before lowering his lips to hers at last. John kissed her like a parched man, drinking water for the first time in days. It was as if all their pent-up longing was transferred into that one long, lingering kiss.

A delicious feeling ran all the way down Evelina's back and into her legs as if her whole body were involved in the kiss. They broke apart, somewhat breathless, and stared into each other's eyes.

"I love you, John."

"You can't imagine how I have longed to hear those words from your lips."

A teasing smile settled on her face. "Maybe I can."

She reached up a hand and ran her fingers over John's hair, and then down the side of his cheek and over the smooth line of his jaw. When her fingers reached his mouth, John captured them with his hand as he leaned toward her and claimed her lips again.

"I love you. I love you. I love you," he said, punctuating each statement with a kiss. "You are far more precious to me than rubies. Never forget it."

And then John kissed her again, just to make sure she had got the message.

EPILOGUE

THREE MONTHS LATER - DECEMBER 1815

*E*velina looked forward to spending Christmas in Duriel Hall. They had been invited to go to her sister's house in Bristol, but John had insisted they remain at home. Even though it meant having the whole family to stay with them instead.

Everyone had arrived—John's parents, his brother's family, and her sister's family. They had all been invited to join them in the drawing room for a cup of tea to refresh them after their journey.

John took Evelina's hand in his own as they sat next to each other on the sofa, waiting for their guests. Philip sat next to them, fidgeting. Evelina guessed he was anxious about meeting her nephews. Richard and Thomas had missed the wedding because they were away at school, so this was their first visit to the Hall. And the first time Philip had met them.

"Nervous?" Evelina asked.

Philip looked up at her, his face lined with worry. "What if they don't like me?"

"There is no point fretting about what you can't control," said John. "This is *your* home. You're the host. It's up to you to make them feel welcome. Can you do that?"

His nephew nodded.

"Good. Now, I just need a few moments with your aunt, so perhaps you can go into the hallway and keep watch. Let us know as soon as our guests come downstairs."

Philip strode out of the room, looking as if he owned it, making Evelina smile. It was amazing how a few well-chosen words could change someone's outlook.

"What was it you wanted to say, my love?"

"I didn't say I wanted to talk to you," John said with a wicked smile as he leaned toward her and stole a kiss. A long kiss. In fact, if Evelina hadn't squeezed his hand, he would still have been kissing her when his sister-in-law breezed through the door.

So much for Philip warning them...

Anne's eyes twinkled with amusement as John pulled away from her. "There is no need to ask whether marriage suits you."

John coloured at his sister-in-law's obvious amusement.

"Wouldn't you agree, Charles?" Anne said to her husband, who had entered the room behind her, carrying their daughter in his arms.

Charles mumbled something that could pass for agreement, then sat down in a chair by the window. He placed Frances on the rug in front of him and picked up a newspaper.

Philip rushed through the door.

"They're coming," he said in an urgent whisper.

"Some of them are already here," John whispered back.

Philip glanced at the other occupants of the room and gave a dismissive grunt. "They're not guests. They're family."

John and Evelina shared an amused smile as Cecilia entered the room, her new babe in her arms, followed by James and his sons.

"Come and sit with us, Cecilia," Anne announced, almost pushing John off the sofa so the three ladies could sit together.

Evelina smiled to herself as John refused to budge until he caught her eye and silently received her approval.

Cecilia sat down between her and Anne, giving Evelina a fine view of her goddaughter. She held out her finger, and the baby wrapped her own tiny fingers around it.

"I can't believe she's nearly a month old," said Evelina.

"And I can't believe you've been married for three months," said her sister.

"I dare you to tell me I didn't do Evelina a good turn, sending her to be Philip's governess," said Anne.

"Are you trying to tell me that was your intent all along?" asked Cecilia.

Anne shrugged. "I thought how agreeable it would be if it happened."

"Mrs Franklin talks as if she engineered the match," Cecilia continued. "She will have it that she was the first person to know of their engagement."

"Was she really, Evelina?"

"I suppose so—but that was our *first* engagement, which, as you both know, came to nothing."

The baby gurgled, drawing their attention back to her. It was not long before the two mothers were exchanging information about their children—a conversation to which Evelina had nothing to contribute.

She glanced over at Philip, who stood behind John, looking most uncomfortable. A second glance showed her that her sister's stepsons looked equally ill at ease.

After dinner, they would play some games with the children, but for now, she thought it would be an excellent idea if they used up some of that energy that boys seemed to have in such plentiful supply.

Evelina excused herself from the other ladies and walked over to where the men stood in conversation. She took Philip aside.

"Why don't you take Richard and Thomas outside?" she said. "Maybe they'd like to see our excavation."

"I don't think they'd be interested."

"You won't know unless you ask."

Philip considered her words, put a brave smile on his face, and approached her nephews. "Would you like to see our Roman mosaic?"

"That doesn't sound very exciting," said Thomas, the older of the two boys.

Evelina's heart sank as Philip's smile faded at the discouraging response. She could see he was about to retreat and shot John an anxious look.

He broke off his conversation and came up behind his nephew.

"Not exciting?" John said. "Don't you like searching for treasure?"

Evelina's nephews eyed him curiously.

"What kind of treasure?" Richard asked.

John shook his head in an exaggerated fashion. "I don't think they want to search for coins, Philip."

"Coins?" said Evelina, her eyes lighting up. "Don't tell me you found coins without me?"

John's eyes shone with amusement. "Very well," he said to Philip, as if saying something confidential, but speaking loud enough for them all to hear. "We won't tell my wife about the coins."

Evelina still glowed with pleasure every time she heard the words 'my wife' on John's tongue.

"We want to search for coins," said Richard. "Don't we, Thomas?"

His brother nodded vigorously.

"Then it sounds like an expedition is in order," said Evelina. "Coats and boots on, if you please. Roman excavations in December are a chilly business."

The children almost ran to the door in their eagerness, with John and Evelina close behind.

"Are you leaving us?" asked Anne, who was rocking her daughter asleep in her arms.

"Yes," said John. "The boys want to see our mosaic."

"And you're going with them, rather than staying to converse with the adults?"

"Yes."

"But you don't even like children, John," she exclaimed. "You always said—"

"As for you, sister," Cecilia chipped in. "You said—"

"In such cases as these," Evelina said, recalling a line from an excellent book she had read, "a good memory is unpardonable."

"Indeed," said John, "and, God willing"—he leaned

over and stroked baby Frances's cheek and then raised his eyes to meet Evelina's gaze—"it won't be long before the master of the Hall has a babe of his own."

Before their family had recovered from the shock of his words, John whisked Evelina out of the room, closing the door behind them.

Evelina bit her lip, her face alight with laughter.

John's face mirrored her own amusement, but then it faded as his eyes grew warm, and he lifted a hand to her cheek. Taking advantage of the empty hallway, John leaned in and claimed her lips with his own.

DID YOU LIKE IT?

I hope you enjoyed reading *Engaging Miss Shaw*.

If you did, please consider leaving a rating and/or review on Amazon, BookBub or Goodreads, because this encourages me and helps other readers to find my stories.

Thank you.

READING GROUP RESOURCES

Would you like to enjoy this book with your reading group? The *Hearts of the Hall* novellas each come with reading group resources.

Visit **heartsofthehall.com/reading** to download your discussion questions for *Engaging Miss Shaw* and the other books in the series.

GLOSSARY

Engaging Miss Shaw refers to two people you will not find in the history books—Mr Westlake and Lord Harting. They are both characters from *The Merry Romances*.

Mr Westlake was the beloved, deceased father of Alicia Westlake, the heroine of *A Perfect Match*. He was a keen classical scholar and a talented artist with a special interest in the excavations at Pompeii.

The Lord Harting referred to is Christopher Merry, 5th Earl of Harting. He first appears as plain Mr Merry, the hero of *A Perfect Match*. He is also a keen classical scholar and an expert on the excavations at Pompeii and Herculaneum.

Bath: The biggest city in Somerset, famous for its hot springs and its Roman baths. It was a fashionable spa town in the 18th century when people came to drink the waters in the Pump Room. Many of the buildings date from this time, including those in the Circus (where John's parents lived) and the Royal Crescent. By the Regency, it was less popular because of the new fashion for the seaside.

Battledore and shuttlecock: A children's game similar to badminton played with small racquets called battledores.

Bow Street Runner: The Bow Street Runners were a professional police force established in Bow Street, London, by magistrate Henry Fielding in 1749. People outside London could request their help to track down offenders.

Breakfast: The first meal of the day, but not the first activity. Typically, people were up for an hour or two before gathering for breakfast.

Breeched: Dressed in breeches or trousers. In the Georgian period, boys were dressed in petticoats until they were breeched, usually between the ages of four and seven, after which they wore men's clothes.

Circus: A ring of Georgian townhouses in Bath designed by John Wood, the Elder.

Dinnertime: Dinner was the chief meal of the day. During the Regency, people ate at different times, from as early as four to as late as nine o'clock. The time depended on many factors, such as class, whether you were in the town or the country, whether you had visitors, and how fashionable you were.

Dowry: The money, goods or estate settled on a woman which she brings to her husband on their marriage.

Drawing room: Short for withdrawing room. Ladies retired to the drawing room after dinner, leaving the gentlemen at the table to imbibe stronger drinks, such as port. It was the sitting room where the gentry received visitors.

Duriel: A Hebrew name meaning 'God is my home'.

Eton: A public boarding school in Berkshire where the gentry and aristocracy sent their sons to be educated. Boys could attend from as young as five, but it was more normal to start school at about thirteen years old.

Gig: A two-wheeled carriage, driven by its owner, and usually pulled by a single horse.

Gunter's: A fashionable tea shop in Berkeley Square, London, famous for its ice creams.

Half-boots: Flat, ankle-high boots that laced up at the front or the side.

Herculaneum: An ancient seaside town in Campania, Italy, that was buried under volcanic ash when Mount Vesuvius erupted in 79 AD. It was fashionable to visit the excavations at Herculaneum during the Grand Tour.

Hessians: A man's riding boot, which was fashionable in the Regency period.

Icehouse: During the winter, ice and snow were collected—typically from a frozen lake—and stored in an icehouse. Straw and sawdust were used to help insulate this ice, which was then used throughout the rest of the year to keep things cool.

Jack Robinson: The expression 'before you can say Jack Robinson' means a very short time. The expression is mentioned in Grose's *A Classical Dictionary of the Vulgar Tongue* (1785).

Jackstraws: A children's game played with straws. The object is to pick up as many as possible from a pile of straws without moving the others.

Luncheon: A handful of food or a light repast between mealtimes.

Marriage licence: There were two types of marriage licence—a common licence and a special licence. Most people were married in their parish church after the banns had been read for three prior Sundays. If a couple wanted to marry more quickly, they could get a common licence from a bishop or archbishop which enabled them to marry immediately. This is the type of licence John planned to get from the bishop's office in Wells.

A special licence was much rarer and more expensive and could only be issued by the Archbishop of Canterbury. It allowed the couple to marry anywhere and at any time.

Merlin swings: The attractions advertised in Sydney Gardens in Bath in 1815 included Merlin swings, designed by an eccentric inventor called John-Joseph Merlin (1735–1803). A contemporary map of the labyrinth suggests that at least one Merlin swing was in the centre of the maze. No consistent description of these swings exists, but some illustrations of what are thought to be Merlin swings suggest they worked like a modern-day swing boat at a fairground. I have used these images to describe how the Merlin swings may have looked.

Morning call: Short visits of ceremony paid to your acquaintances. Despite the name, they were normally made in the afternoon, between one and four o'clock.

Napoleon: Napoleon Bonaparte (1760–1821) was a French military leader who fought against the allied armies led by the British. He was defeated by the Duke of Wellington at the Battle of Waterloo in June 1815.

Norwich shawl: A luxurious type of dress shawl made in Norwich, Norfolk. Made of a silk and wool mix, they imitated the expensive shawls imported from India.

Nuncheon: Food eaten between meals. When dinner was at midday, a nuncheon might be eaten between dinner and supper. By the Regency, dinner was eaten well into the afternoon or evening, so a nuncheon or luncheon might be eaten around midday to sustain a person between breakfast and dinner.

Pelisse: A long fitted coat.

Pompeii: An ancient city near Naples, Italy, which was covered by volcanic ash when Mount Vesuvius erupted in AD 79. It was fashionable to visit the excavations at Pompeii during the Grand Tour.

Pride and Prejudice: A novel in three volumes by Jane Austen, published in 1813. When it first appeared in print, it was 'by the author of *Sense and Sensibility*', which in turn was written 'by a lady'. Evelina quotes from *Pride and Prejudice* in the epilogue.

Regency: The Regency period was the nine years from 1811 to 1820 when the Prince of Wales, the future George IV, ruled as Prince Regent during the last illness of his father, George III.

Reticule: A lady's purse or small bag designed to carry around personal items that used to be kept in a pocket. Pockets became impractical when dresses became more streamlined, and so a reticule acted like a portable pocket.

Royal Crescent: A crescent-shaped row of Georgian townhouses in Bath designed by the architect John Wood the Younger.

Sea bathing: Sea bathing became popular during the second half of the 18th century when two eminent doctors, Dr Russell and Dr Crane, recommended it to their wealthy clients as an aid to good health. They recommended drinking seawater as well as bathing in it. Popular seaside resorts included Weymouth and Brighton.

Smallpox: A serious, contagious disease which was fatal in around a third of cases where the patient had not been inoculated. Survivors of the disease were often covered with scars and could go blind.

Spencer jacket: A short-waisted jacket that ended just under the bosom.

Stagecoach: A large, closed carriage with four wheels used for public transport, pulled by four or six horses.

Steward: A person appointed to manage another's affairs, such as their estate.

Sweet on someone: To be sweet on someone is first recorded in the 1690s.

Sydney Gardens: Pleasure gardens in Bath. Also known as Sydney Garden Vauxhall, as the gardens sought to emulate the famous Vauxhall pleasure gardens. The gardens boasted groves, vistas, lawns, serpentine walks, shady bowers, waterfalls, alcoves, bowling greens, Merlin swings, grottoes and labyrinths. Entry was by subscription season ticket or pay per visit.

Tessera (plural tesserae): A small block of stone, tile, glass, or other hard material used in the construction of a mosaic. They came in various colours.

Tidbit: A small piece of interesting information or gossip. Also titbit (UK).

Waterloo: The Battle of Waterloo, fought on 18 June 1815, was the decisive battle which ended the Napoleonic wars. The allied armies, led by the Duke of Wellington, were victorious.

Waters—taking the waters: People visited spa towns like Bath to drink the mineral waters which were supposed to be beneficial to their health.

Wellington: Arthur Wellesley, Duke of Wellington (1769–1852), was a British military leader and British Prime Minister. He led the allied armies to victory at the Battle of Waterloo, ending the Napoleonic wars.

Weymouth: A fashionable seaside resort which rose to importance through the repeated visits of King George III. Its sheltered bay made it suitable for sea bathing all year round.

AUTHOR'S NOTE

Writing can be a lonely occupation, and finding other writers you can share your joys and frustrations with is an incredible blessing. My fantastic online writer support group was founded during the Covid lockdown of 2020 with fellow Christian authors Philippa Jane Keyworth and Edwina Kiernan. As our author names all begin with the letter K, we refer to ourselves as the K-team. We have been supporting and encouraging one another in our writing and in our lives ever since.

The *Hearts of the Hall* series was conceived in 2021 in one of our online meet-ups. We thought it would be fun to write a series together, showing three generations of the same family, in the same house. My thanks go to Philippa and Edwina for their ongoing love and support and for their invaluable feedback on my draft manuscript.

The historical detail and language used in the novel are as accurate as I could make them based on my research at the time of writing.

Special thanks go to Andrew, my wonderful husband and editor, for his love, patience and encouragement.

ABOUT THE AUTHOR

Rachel Knowles writes faith-based Regency romance.

She first read Jane Austen's *Pride and Prejudice* at the age of thirteen and fell in love, not only with Mr Darcy, but with the entire Regency period.

Since 2011, she has been blogging about her research on her website: **RegencyHistory.net**. She also writes historical non-fiction based on her extensive research.

Rachel lives in the beautiful Georgian seaside town of Weymouth in Dorset, on the south coast of England, with her husband, Andrew. They have four grown-up daughters and a growing number of grandchildren.

amazon.com/author/rachelknowles

bookbub.com/authors/rachel-knowles

goodreads.com/rachelknowles

instagram.com/rachelknowlesauthor

twitter.com/RegencyHistory

facebook.com/RegencyHistory

ALSO BY RACHEL KNOWLES

THE MERRY ROMANCES

A Perfect Match

https://mybook.to/APM

A Reason For Romance

https://mybook.to/ARFR

WHAT REGENCY WOMEN DID FOR US

Historical Non-Fiction

Be inspired by the stories of twelve Regency women, from very different backgrounds, who helped change the world they lived in and whose legacy is still evident today. These women were pioneers, philanthropists and entrepreneurs, authors, scientists and actresses—women who made an impact on their world and ours.

https://mybook.to/WRWDFU

NEWSLETTER

Want to read more by Rachel and be the first to hear about book bargains and giveaways?

Sign up to her newsletter at:

RegencyHistory.net

FINDING MISS GILES

Book 1 in the Hearts of the Hall series

She's yearning for a family and a home. He's keeping a promise to find her.

Bath, 1780: Without family or fortune, Miss Araminta Giles must rely on her wit alone.

Engaged by Mr Derringer to be companion to his sister for the Bath Season, Ary views this position as merely another in a line of employments necessary to her survival.

So when she finds herself warming to Charlotte, and shivering under the intense gaze of Mr Derringer, she is surprised to find herself hoping for more than just a roof over her head. But a series of intriguing encounters in polite Society cause Ary to realise her position with the Derringers may not be the fruit of her own labours after all. As she tries to make sense of the revelations, she is forced to consider what she really wants.

Will she keep going through life relying only on herself? Or is she willing to take a chance on a home, family and... love?

heartsofthehall.com/findingmissgiles

RESTORING MISS HASTINGS

Book 3 in the Hearts of the Hall series

Devastated by loss... a stranger takes her in. But will her presence ruin his plans to restore all he's lost?

Harriet Hastings has nowhere left to turn: after losing both her parents within a few months of each other, she is penniless and alone. So when a distant relative makes arrangements for her future, Harriet faces another loss — leaving the place she calls home to go and live with strangers.

Edmund Derringer's on a mission: to restore the family heirlooms he pawned to cover the debts of his failed speculation. The last thing he needs is to be saddled with his cousin's ward — a friendly chatterbox who intrudes on his time, distracting him from the task at hand.

But when outside forces threaten their burgeoning fondness, each will be compelled to re-examine what they really believe about one another, and what their most important goal for the future truly is...

heartsofthehall.com/restoringmisshastings

Printed in Great Britain
by Amazon

10465069R00164